W9-BCC-171

A NECESSARY END

No one at first connected the body found by a lonely country road with Nancy Pendrick, the career wife of a hotel owner in the village of Frecklemarsh and head of her own London cookery school. After all, Nancy had insisted on returning to London after the New Year holiday, pleading pressure of work, no one had reported her missing. So what was she doing back in Broadshire? Her husband could offer no explanation so Chief Inspector Webb sets out grimly to find the killer.

Books by Anthea Fraser
in the Ulverscroft Large Print Series:

A SHROUD FOR DELILAH
A NECESSARY END

ANTHEA FRASER

A NECESSARY END

Complete and Unabridged

ULVERSCROFT
Leicester

First published in Great Britain in 1985 by
William Collins Sons & Co. Ltd.,
London & Glasgow

First Large Print Edition
published December 1986
by arrangement with
William Collins Sons & Co. Ltd.,
London & Glasgow
and
Walker & Company Inc.,
New York

British Library CIP Data

Fraser, Anthea
    A necessary end.—Large print ed.—
    Ulverscroft large print series: mystery
    I. Title
    823′.914[F]   PR6056.R28/

    ISBN 0-7089-1555-8

Published by
F. A. Thorpe (Publishing) Ltd.
Anstey, Leicestershire
Set by Rowland Phototypesetting Ltd.
Bury St. Edmunds, Suffolk
Printed and bound in Great Britain by
T. J. Press (Padstow) Ltd., Padstow, Cornwall

For IMF, with love.

'Death, a necessary end . . .'
SHAKESPEARE: *Julius Caesar*

1

"NOT much further now!" Roger said, and immediately despised himself for the false heartiness in his voice. Faith merely nestled deeper into her furs. She felt the cold regardless of temperature, and managed to imply it was Roger's fault. Yet it had been a mild Christmas and the unseasonable weather seemed set to continue over New Year.

How different it had been in his childhood, with snow falling as he and Avis sang carols with the Yates girls. Briefly he thought of Charlotte, the love of his youth and, like his sister, an integral part of Christmas Past along with mistletoe and stockings and the huge Christmas tree, whose pungent smell of the forest lent enchantment to the whole house. Faith's only concession to the season was a pseudo-tree in the hall, a sterile mockery of the spicy ghosts of the past.

"Let me put the fairy on top!" Avis cried in his head, and his hands tightened

1

on the wheel. Oh God, Avis, why did you die like that?

Catching an echo of his thoughts, Faith stirred, looking without interest at the rich fields bordering the motorway. "I can't think why you insisted on coming," she remarked in her high voice. "It was different when Avis was alive, but you've little in common with the rest of them."

"They're the only family I have," he answered steadily. "My sister's children."

"But not your sister's husband. Not any more."

Was she trying to hurt him? Probably not, but she had. That remarriage barely a year later still rankled, nor did his legal brain grant mitigating circumstances. Certainly not the children, at twenty and sixteen past the need for a surrogate mother; nor, unless Oliver had deceived himself, provision for companionship.

Again Faith broke in on his thoughts. "Though he can hardly feel married, with Nancy in London all the time."

"A weekend wife," Roger agreed. "But since it's lasted three years, it must be working."

"Perhaps," said Faith with a laugh, "he

2

hoped to transport her and her culinary arts to The Gables!" Oliver was the proprietor of a small but highly thought of hotel in Broadshire, which drew its clients from as far afield as Europe and America.

"He'd have had staff problems if he'd tried!" Roger rejoined.

"Who do you suppose will provide the food tonight?"

"Nancy, almost certainly. On New Year's Eve they'll be fully booked. They won't have time to ferry stuff across to the Lodge."

The Shillingham exit loomed on their left and he moved into the slow lane. "We'll just about make it in daylight," he said with satisfaction.

"But you must stay! I've accepted the invitation."

Nancy Pendrick wiped her hands down her apron. "It's your own fault, Oliver. You should have checked with me first."

"I naturally thought you'd be here all week. Damn it, the Beresfords are staying till Thursday. You can't waltz off when there are guests in the house."

3

"They're your guests, not mine, and Mrs. Foldes will cope admirably."

"For all her attributes," Oliver said tartly, "Mrs. Foldes wasn't engaged as wife-substitute."

Nancy flushed and picked up a knife, beginning the rapid slicing of a pile of radishes. "I can't make drinks on Tuesday, but I'll be back on Friday for the Bartletts. Even that's pushing it; it's a short week already, with Monday a Bank Holiday."

"But why go at all? The school's closed till the sixteenth."

"But Dean's Catering isn't. I should really go back on Monday, but provided I can make an early start, I'll stay till Tuesday."

"How accommodating of you."

Her anger rose to meet his. "Look, Oliver, if you'd wanted a wife to darn socks and put out your slippers, you chose the wrong one. You knew my career was important to me."

"But I thought I was, too. Damn it, I didn't ask you to give up work, but I expected *some* consideration. Now, you even grudge me the weekends."

4

The kitchen door opened before she could reply. She made herself say levelly, "I've almost finished in here. Have you set out the drinks?"

"I'll see to them now." Passing his son in the doorway, Oliver left the room. Henry came in and Nancy smacked his hand as he reached for a canapé.

"No filching, or there won't be enough to go round."

"Can you spare me a moment?"

She turned to look at him. Henry, like his sister, favoured his mother's side of the family. Though as tall as Oliver, he was of slimmer build and instead of his father's thick chestnut hair, his was that rich honey-gold which characterized the Beresfords.

"As long as it really is a moment. Your uncle and aunt will be here soon and I must go and change."

"I'll make it brief, then." He wasn't meeting her eye and curiosity checked her impatience. Oliver's children didn't usually seek her out.

"Well?"

He said in a rush, "I was wondering if you'd lend me some money."

5

She lent back against the counter, folding her arms and studying his averted face. "Why?"

"Because I—need it."

"Don't be an idiot, Henry. Of course you need it, or you wouldn't have asked. My question was, why?"

He coloured, an adolescent bane he'd not outgrown. "I owe it to someone."

"Go on."

"Well, to tell the truth, I put some money on a horse."

"And lost it, I presume. Let that be a lesson to you. But why me? Why not see your father?"

"He said he wouldn't help out again."

So Oliver knew the boy was gambling. He hadn't mentioned it to her, but then he never discussed his children. "You'll have to pay it back a bit at a time, then, won't you?"

"But it's been going on several weeks already. They're getting impatient."

"What kind of money are we talking about?" She had fifty pounds in her handbag. Provided it taught him a lesson, she didn't mind standing surety. But his reply astounded her.

6

"Five hundred."

"*Five hundred?* I can't rustle that up at the drop of a ˙ hat, and if I could, I wouldn't. If it's that serious, you'll have to brave Oliver."

Henry said rapidly, "I don't quite know how to say this, but I heard you talking to Dad once, soon after you were married." His face was scarlet. Nancy watched him in silence, wondering what was coming. "You were discussing Wills, because of the marriage and everything. And you said—I couldn't help hearing—I was in the kitchen, and the hatch was open. You said as you'd no children of your own, you'd leave lump sums to Rose and me."

She recalled the conversation. Her proposal had been more to placate Oliver for her staying in London than out of affection for his offspring, who from the first had treated her with studied indifference.

"So all I'm asking, really, is for my share now. I know it's a cheek, but I—I thought perhaps you wouldn't mind, since I need it so badly."

"Then you were mistaken," Nancy said crisply. His attempt to turn eavesdropping to advantage disgusted her and she'd lost all patience with him.

"Nancy, for God's sake—"

"Not for anyone's sake. You must speak to your father, but I'd advise you to wait till tomorrow. He's enough on his plate at the moment."

Henry spun round and slammed out of the room. These bloody Pendricks! Now she'd antagonized another of them. Last month it had been Rose. As if it was her fault that stupid boy had fallen for her. Sympathy at Rose's treatment of him was no licence for the wet kiss he'd planted on her mouth. It would have been laughable if Rose hadn't come in on it, but the resulting charge of enticement was not pleasant.

Rose at nineteen was a disturbing mix of *femme fatale* and little girl. Recently, the spoilt child had been uppermost, and she'd adopted an annoying air of "I know something you don't know." Nancy hadn't gratified her by showing curiosity, but she did wonder what revenge she proposed to take. And as if all that wasn't enough, Danny'd shown up at the hotel. Was it any wonder she escaped to London?

8

God! Was that the time? And the *vol-au-vents* still had to be filled. Dismissing her family and its problems, Nancy set to work.

Charlotte Yates, sipping her wine at the far end of the room, caught sight of Roger before he saw her, and smiled to herself. Dear Roger—how little he'd changed! He still had that worried small-boy look she had once found so endearing, and the lock of hair fell as it always had over his forehead. Even the hesitant manner and apologetic smile were the same.

She felt a rush of warmth for him, embodying as he did the hopes and dreams of her youth; and the tragedies, too. It was to Roger she'd run when her guinea-pig died, just as, years later, she'd turned to him during her father's last illness. And he in turn had confided in her all his ambitions for the future. What had gone wrong? Why, when as a mere formality he'd asked her to marry him, had she stunned them both by refusing?

With an effort, Charlotte shook off her nostalgia. He should be grateful, she told herself briskly, that she had. The Honourable Faith de Courcy had done more for his career than she could, and Roger had always been ambitious. Now a Queen's Counsel, his name appeared regularly in all the big murder trials. No doubt, she reflected ironically, that charming diffidence disarmed the opposition.

He'd seen her now, and, his hand under Faith's elbow, was coming towards her.

"Charlotte, hello!" She held out her cheek for his kiss. "Lovely to see you! How is everyone? Valerie still in Canada?"

"Yes indeed. She hopes to come over next summer."

"Her daughter must be grown up now. What was her name?"

"Hannah. She came back some years ago, and has a flat in Shillingham. In fact, I'm staying with her for the weekend."

Roger moved closer and lowered his voice. "Talking of old times, guess who I saw in the hall just now."

"Surprise me."

"Heather Jarvis. At least, Heather Jarvis that was."

"Really? Good Lord!"

"I don't think she recognized me. I never knew her well."

Faith spoke for the first time. "Wasn't she engaged to Oliver, before he met Avis?"

"*When* he met Avis," Roger corrected significantly.

"Well, what's so surprising? In London, one's always coming across permutations of ex-husbands and wives."

Charlotte said, "I thought Heather'd married some doctor and gone to live up north?"

Nancy, approaching with a bottle of wine, refilled her glass. "Heather Frayne? Yes, she did, but they've moved back. Ivor Cudlip's enlarging his practice and Peter applied. He wanted to come because his mother's been ill. If you know Heather, do go and have a word with them. They don't know many people yet."

Roger and Faith moved obediently away, but Charlotte lingered a moment. "Remember offering me your London flat for a weekend?"

"Yes, of course. Any time."

"Would next weekend be convenient? I'd enjoy a look round the sales."

"Certainly. It'll be free from Friday lunch-time. Remind me before you go and I'll give you a key, in case we miss each other."

Oliver too had seen the Fraynes and he braced himself to speak to them. He'd have preferred not to invite them at all, but with the Cudlips on the guest list, the omission would have been too pointed. And he'd only himself to blame if he was less than comfortable in Heather's company.

God, what a mess everything was! Avis dead, he and Nancy snapping at each other, and then, out of the blue, Heather of all people returning to Frecklemarsh. It was only now, seeing her after all these years, that he fully realized how badly he'd treated her. At the time, his passion for Avis had blinded him to everything.

Well, it hadn't brought him much happiness. With hindsight he might have done better to stick with Heather and let his infatuation burn itself out. Still, it was water under the bridge now. He could only hope she'd found the happiness that eluded him. Across the room, he studied her husband, unimpressed by what he saw. Though good-looking enough, Frayne's mouth had a petulant droop and he'd made short work of that first drink.

With a carefully arranged smile on his face, Oliver went to greet them.

Rose looked ravishing tonight, Roger thought. There was a glitter about her that reminded him achingly of her mother, and the movement of her body under the tight dress was drawing male eyes from all round the room. Yet despite her beauty, he mourned the small girl she had been, laughing and pouting and winding him round her little finger.

"Want Uncle to put me to bed!" she'd say, and he'd smiling comply. There'd be no shortage of volunteers now: he could only hope she'd be more circumspect than her mother in accommodating them.

He walked over to her, leaving Faith with the local architect, and slipped an arm round her waist. "How's my favourite girl?"

She smiled at him, threading his arm through hers. "Come and dance!"

The dining-area, its rugs removed, had

been cleared for dancing, and Henry and his girlfriend were manning the record-player. Roger said facetiously, "I'm grateful you can spare time for elderly relatives!"

"I've always time for you, Uncle. Anyway, I'm between men at the moment. It's quite a relief."

"The chap in the corner looks ready to step in."

"Oh, I can't be bothered with *boys*! Give me older men every time, even if they do get too intense."

Roger felt an obscure alarm. "Rose, you will be careful, won't you? I don't want you hurt, my darling."

"I shan't be. It wasn't me who got serious. Still, it was fun while it lasted, a kind of tit-for-tat, though he didn't realize."

"Tit-for-tat? What do you mean?"

"Darling Uncle, stop worrying! I can take care of myself!"

The music changed and she spun out of his arms, twisting and shaking with the abandonment of youth and well aware of the notice she was attracting. Feeling ridiculous, Roger danced sedately opposite

14

her. She was up to something and he didn't like the sound of it. Oh, why did she have to grow up? She'd been such a sweet little girl.

It was midnight. Big Ben rang out over the stereo and they joined hands for "Auld Lang Syne". Oliver dutifully kissed his wife, his daughter, and the two or three women between him and the kitchen. Then, extricating himself, he continued on his way to fetch the champagne. It was only when he'd rounded the fridge that he realized the room wasn't empty. Heather had turned from the sink, a glass of water in her hand.

His first instinct was to mutter an apology and withdraw. He resisted it, made himself smile. "You missed the celebrations!"

"I don't care for that part very much."

He'd forgotten how large and dark her eyes were, and her habit, surprisingly rare, of keeping them steadily on one as she spoke. "But you'll let me wish you Happy New Year, I hope?"

She smiled slightly. "Happier than the last one you wished me?"

He was taken aback. She was prepared to talk about it, then. For himself, he'd have preferred a social gloss-over. He said stiffly, "I behaved very badly. I hope you've forgiven me."

"Of course. Years ago."

She was more attractive than he remembered. No fires had been lit by their love-making in those pre-permissive days—it had taken Avis to do that. Now, though, he felt a growing excitement to which his mood contributed—irritation with Nancy, the drinks he'd had, the volatile time of year. Hell, it was a night for kissing and he suddenly needed to kiss her.

"Happy New Year, Heather."

The note in his voice alerted her, and her startled look changed to an answering awareness. They came together awkwardly, clumsily, but at the moment of contact their bodies fused in a shuddering acknowledgment of desire, succumbing helplessly to a passion as devastating as it was unexpected. It could have lasted only seconds before Heather pulled away.

And as they stood panting, staring at each other, a voice from the door said,

"Oh, there you are, Mrs. Frayne. I'm afraid your husband's not well. Would you like us to take him home?"

With a cry of distress, Heather hurried from the room. Oliver stood where she'd left him, his mouth dry and his heart clattering against his ribs. Beside him, the fridge clicked and roared, the cold tap dripped into the sink.

"Dear God in heaven!" he said aloud. "What happens now?"

An hour later, Rose shivered in her bedroom as she read the letter again:

What do you mean, its over? What are you doing to me? For Gods sake Rose you know how I feel about you. Its taken me a lifetime to find you so stop teasing there's a good girl. I made you happy didn't I? And I'll go on making you happy I swear it. If its your father and Nancy you're worried about forget it. I'll sort things out. Meet me at the usual place on Sunday. If you're not there I'll come and get you. I love you my darling. Now and for ever.

She drew a deep breath and began to tear the paper into fragments. Then she swept them into her hand, held them over the waste basket and let them fall in a snow-storm of flakes.

"Happy Bloody New Year!" she said.

Roger came through from the bathroom, fastening his pyjama jacket.

"It was a good party, wasn't it? Glad we came after all?"

"Yes, I quite enjoyed it." Faith wasn't given to overstatement. She was standing at the dressing-table in her silk nightgown, brushing her short, expertly-cut hair. He came up behind her, his eyes on hers in the mirror, and saw their guardedness. God! he screamed silently. Why won't she let me touch her? He turned away, feeling her relax.

"The only thing that spoiled it," she went on after a moment, "was that doctor making a fool of himself. I was sorry for his wife."

"He probably needed to relax, poor chap. Drink's an occupational hazard with medics."

"Hardly reassuring for prospective

patients." She laid her brush down and reached for the jar of night-cream. "That Charlotte of yours is an odd character, isn't she? I mean, smoking cigars and those extraordinary clothes. Sheer affectation, surely?"

It occurred to neither of them that Faith speaking of affectation was the supreme irony.

Roger hesitated, unwilling for a complexity of reasons to discuss Charlotte with his wife. "It's not a pose. She's genuinely not interested in what people think of her."

"Did you say she lectures at Oxford? That might account for it!" Faith's father and brothers were Cambridge men. "However, the person who really alarmed me was Rose. It was like watching Avis all over again."

Roger sobered. "Yes, I know. I tried to speak to her, but of course she wouldn't listen."

Faith ran a finger over the creases in his forehead. "You can't solve everyone's problems, my love. Leave that young lady to her father."

He caught and held her hand, despite

19

her attempt to free it. "You do love me, don't you, Faith?"

"Darling, what a question!"

"Do you?"

"Of course I do. Now let go of my hand. I'm tired and I want to go to sleep." She kissed his cheek and slid between the sheets, pointedly closing her eyes.

Roger sighed, walked to the window and held back the curtain. Beyond the narrow garden lay the main road through the village. Across it and slightly to his right, he could make out the gateway to The Gables, though the building was hidden by trees. He could hear music in the distance; no doubt the festivities would last all night.

At the sound of footsteps, he looked down in time to see Henry turn into the drive and disappear round the side of the house. Walked his girlfriend home, no doubt. Wise of Oliver to ban cars for the evening and let the kids invite their own guests.

Roger dropped the curtain and looked over at the bed. Eyes closed and breathing regularly, Faith gave the impression of sleep. Message received!

20

Still in the time-warp of New Year, his mind slipped back to the early days when, warm and demonstrative by nature, he'd been hurt by his wife's reserve. Their lovemaking she accepted as her duty, but a touch on her hand, an arm round her shoulders, made her shy like a nervous thoroughbred. Which, of course, she was, he conceded ruefully.

And before he could stop them, his thoughts turned back to Charlotte. Seeing her again had unsettled him. There was still pain in remembering those early days, though how much of it stemmed from their association with Avis, he wasn't sure. But they'd had something, he and Charlotte, a closeness, a oneness of thought that he'd never achieved with Faith. Why had she let it go? Did she ever regret it, as he did?

He sighed, his eyes refocusing on the quiet figure in the bed. Still, Faith was a good wife according to her lights. His homes were run smoothly, his comfort always their top priority, and there was no doubt she was an asset socially, the perfect hostess, the sought-after guest. Furthermore, her connections had done a lot for

21

his career, in which she was intensely interested. Now he could repay her, with the knighthood attendant on a High Court Judge. That goal, the focal point of his hopes for as long as he could remember, was at last within his grasp.

Carefully, so as not to disturb his wife, Roger climbed into bed and prepared himself to sleep.

2

"SO tell me about the party!" Hannah invited, setting down the coffee tray. "Did you meet any ghosts from the past?"

Charlotte smiled. "More than one, yes. It was most enjoyable."

"I hadn't realized you knew the second wife."

"It was I who introduced them. It makes me feel responsible, which I resent."

"But they're happy, aren't they?"

"I hope so." Charlotte sipped her coffee. "There was an unpleasant atmosphere last night. I'd the feeling they'd had a blazing row before we arrived and couldn't wait for us to go, so they could get on with it. Oliver was very tight-lipped at the beginning."

She paused, and added reflectively, "Although I introduced them, it never occurred to me I was playing Cupid. Oliver'd phoned to say he was in London,

23

and as I was lunching with Nancy, I asked him to join us. Then, when we came out of the restaurant, it was raining. They were going in the same direction, so they shared a taxi. I thought no more about it till Nancy phoned a few weeks later to say they were getting married. I was— astounded."

Hannah refilled her cup. "Why was it so surprising?"

"Because I knew she'd never leave London. She's founder-president of the Nancy Dean School of Cookery and runs a profitable catering firm on the side, which sends meals to directors' dining-rooms and so on. She wasn't likely to pull up stakes to vegetate in Frecklemarsh. Nor was there any chance of Oliver selling The Gables and moving to London. And Nancy'd told me once she felt much freer doing her own thing without a husband round her neck. Though from what I gather, Danny Dean would have been a drag on anyone."

"You've never met him?"

"No, they'd split up when I met Nancy, but they still keep in touch. 'Touch' being the operative word," Charlotte added drily. "He's not above asking for money on occasion. He's never stuck at a job in his life, which was why Nancy had to support them. She started very modestly by cooking for dinner parties, and it grew from there."

"Where's Danny now?"

Charlotte shrugged. "On his feet, I don't doubt. He wheedles his way into one job after another, gets bored, and moves on, leaving his employer high and dry. He must have the charm of the devil to get away with it."

"No doubt Oliver's first marriage was more orthodox."

Charlotte was silent, staring into the fire.

"Well?" Hannah prompted. "Don't tell me there are skeletons in his closet, too!"

"He and Avis certainly weren't orthodox. Their marriage started with a bang, swung badly off the rails—or at least, Avis did—and ended in tragedy."

"She went off the rails? How do you mean? I thought you liked her?"

"I loved her," Charlotte said simply. "We all did, but that didn't stop me wanting to shake her. She was beautiful and vivacious and witty, but she was supremely selfish. All that mattered was that she got what she wanted. And she wanted Oliver. No matter that he was about to marry Heather Jarvis. Avis set her cap at him and he fell for her, hook, line and sinker. It was almost ludicrous to see. So we went to the wedding and sat back to see what would happen. And what happened was that she got bored.

"It was understandable, of course. Oliver hadn't time to dance attendance on her. His father, who'd started The Gables, had just handed over to him and he was working all hours. And as they lived in the hotel, she'd nothing to occupy her, which was fatal. I think that's why she had a child straight away. But caring for a baby soon lost its novelty. During my vacations she was always on the phone, wanting me to go for drives, to concerts and exhibitions—anything, just to get out of the hotel."

"Didn't Oliver see what was happening?"

"If he did, there was little he could do. The Gables was beginning to repay his hard work and had to be nursed along.

But when Avis became pregnant again, he asked Jeff Bartlett to convert three cottages across the road and they moved over there."

"Did she settle, once she'd a place of her own?"

"I'm afraid not. By that time I'd moved to Oxford permanently and didn't see so much of them. But I heard she'd hired a nanny and was spending a lot of time with Faith and Roger. She was seen with prominent people in fashionable places, and inevitably there was talk. She was even cited in a divorce case, but Oliver was still besotted with her and believed her when she protested her innocence. Or at least, he pretended to. He probably felt if her affairs were the price he had to pay to keep her, then he'd accept them. But they began to have rows. Quite often Avis would start one in public, and it was highly embarrassing all round. And she got progressively less discreet. Believe it or not, she even brought an occasional man back with her and booked him into the hotel! She was drinking, too. All the classic symptoms of a bored, unhappy woman, though God knows she'd two lovely children and a husband who adored her. And by this time the strain was showing on Oliver, too."

Charlotte stopped speaking, lost in her thoughts. After a moment, Hannah said softly, "What was the tragedy you mentioned? I forget the details."

"One night she came home slightly the worse for drink, tripped over her long dress, and fell backwards down the stairs. She broke her neck."

"How appalling! Poor Oliver."

"Yes. It emerged later that she'd been with one of her lovers. They were seen in a car parked outside a country club. I confess that at the time—"

"Yes? At the time, what?"

Charlotte looked up. "Don't dare repeat this to that policeman of yours, but I did wonder if Oliver was waiting at the top of the stairs, and if perhaps—only perhaps— he might have given her the teeniest push."

Hannah stared at her. "You're saying he might have *murdered* her?"

"Certainly not!" Charlotte spoke sharply. "Though God knows he'd enough provocation. If—just *if* she was tipsy enough to taunt him with her evening's entertainment, well, one could hardly blame him. It wouldn't be murder, more a *crime passionel*."

"It would be murder in my book," Hannah said flatly, "and in David's, too. No, of course I won't tell him, but I hope you kept your wild theories to yourelf." She paused, then asked with interest, "How did Oliver take it?"

"He was devastated. He convinced himself their life had been idyllic—another reason for my surprise when he remarried. After all, it was barely a year later. And Nancy's so different from Avis, in character and appearance. She seems quite out of place at the Lodge—small, brown Nancy and the tall, golden Pendricks. Like a sparrow among peacocks." Charlotte reached for her handbag. "Do you mind if I smoke?" It was a rhetorical question and Hannah watched in silence as she lit a slim cigar.

"What happened to the girl Oliver was engaged to?"

Her aunt smiled, blowing a cloud of pungent smoke. "She walked into the room last night, as large as life."

"Good heavens! So they've kissed and made up?"

"As to that, I couldn't say. He kept out of her way."

"Was there anyone else you knew?"

"Roger, of course. The first man who proposed to me."

"How many have since?"

"Quite a few, impudent child, but none I'd give up my independence for. He hasn't changed at all. Nor, for that matter, has Oliver, apart from a few lines round his mouth and a touch of grey over the ears. What a different time-scale we inhabit as we grow older! In twenty-odd years, the Pendrick children have grown from babyhood through schooldays to young adults, changing beyond recognition in the process. Yet here we all are, preserved like flies in amber. Or is that wishful thinking?"

"What of Roger's wife? Is she wearing well?"

"I'd say so. She's an 'Hon', you know. Daughter of a minor earl."

Hannah burst out laughing. "Darling, how wonderfully dismissive! I gather you don't like her?"

30

"I can't decide. She's languid and elegant and as fastidious as a cat. Beautifully dressed, beautifully groomed."

"But?"

"I don't know. Remote, somehow. Behind a screen."

"I must say," Hannah remarked, stretching, "you had a far more interesting time than I did. David was on duty, so I just went to Gwen's. She lives with her old mother, you know. You can imagine how riotous it was, a headmistress and her deputy solemnly toasting each other, with the old lady nodding in the background! No," she added quickly, at Charlotte's bark of laughter, "that's not fair. I thoroughly enjoyed it. We watched the telly and had a delicious supper. I'm very fond of Gwen."

"And you've asked your policeman round this evening, to make up?"

"I wish you wouldn't keep calling him *my* policeman."

"Well, he is, isn't he?"

"Not really, no. He's very much his own man, and I'm happy to leave it that way."

"No chance of wedding bells, then?"

"None. Like you, I value my independence." She smiled. "I asked him to come and meet my maiden aunt. I think he's in for a surprise."

"Let's hope it's a pleasant one," said Charlotte equably.

"If anyone calls round or phones, I'm not in."

Rose stood in the archway, looking defiantly at her family.

"An ambiguous statement," remarked Henry. "Are we to assume you're going out, or simply taking avoiding action?"

"Does it matter? I'm not in if anyone wants me."

"'Anyone' being—?"

"Anyone at all."

"Don't frown, dear," Faith said absently. "You'll get lines on your face. Come and sit down. You make me uneasy, standing there glowering."

Roger put down the local paper. "The play at the Grand gets a good crit. Shall we give it a try? Our treat, of course, to repay your hospitality."

"Nancy won't be here," Oliver said. "Having indulged us with three days of

32

her company, she's off to the bright lights."

Roger looked at his hostess, who'd flushed. "What a shame. I thought you'd be here all week."

"So did the rest of us. It can't be Tuesday, anyway. The Pipers have invited us for drinks. As usual, I had to make Nancy's excuses."

"The price of being indispensable," Roger said peaceably.

"Except that she's not. There's a qualified staff who can cope perfectly well."

"Perhaps you'd let me judge if I'm needed or not," Nancy said angrily. "And you've no room to criticize. You spend all your time at the hotel, leaving your children to fend for themselves. Consequently Rose is out all hours and Henry comes to me with his problems."

Henry jumped to his feet, face flaming. "That's not fair! What I said was in confidence. You've no right to bring it up in public!"

Faith laid aside her embroidery. "Unless everyone stops shouting, I shall go to my room. It's giving me a headache."

"I'm sorry," Roger said. "I started this, by suggesting the theatre."

"Not at all." Oliver spoke brusquely. "It's we who apologize. This has been brewing all weekend, but it's inexcusable to involve you. As to the theatre, the rest of you go ahead, but I'll have to put in an appearance at the hotel on Wednesday. They've been working long hours over the holiday and I must take my turn. In fact, I'll go over now, if you'll excuse me, to check last night's takings. I'll be back in time for lunch."

He left the room without glancing at his wife, and Henry, still on his feet, shot her a venomous look before following him.

"I'm so sorry," Nancy said in a low voice. "That was unforgivable. We've all been rather on edge."

"Happens in the best families," Roger assured her heartily, and didn't notice his wife's raised eyebrows.

Nancy rose to her feet. "I'll go and check on lunch. Rose, perhaps someone would like a drink. See to it, will you?"

Roger put his hand over Rose's and squeezed it. "All right?"

"I suppose so. Thank heaven she's *not*

here any oftener. It's no business of hers how late I stay out. I'm not a child." She drew in her breath. "My God, if she only knew!"

"Knew what, Rosie?"

"Nothing. I'd better do as I'm told and get the drinks. We could all do with one, after that."

In his small, tidy flat, Chief Inspector Webb prepared for his evening out. He'd been up most of the night extracting a confession from a jewel thief, and gone back that morning to clear up the loose ends. Not the best way to celebrate New Year. He felt drained, mentally and physically, and though he wanted to see Hannah, he was sorry her aunt was there. The last thing he felt like was making polite conversation to a thin-ankled, thick-stockinged old lady. Still, with luck she'd retire early with her cocoa. Pulling the door shut behind him, he ran down the stairs to the flat below.

His ring was answered not by Hannah but by a tall, blonde woman, stunningly elegant in oyster silk pyjamas.

"Good evening, Chief Inspector. I'm

35

Charlotte Yates. Do come in. Hannah will be with us in a moment."

He stood staring at her. "You're not—? I mean—"

Her mouth quirked. "Her maiden aunt? Indeed yes. I'm to blame for the phrase, I fear. It's the way I sign my letters."

He smiled ruefully, accepting that he'd been fooled, and Charlotte warmed to him. She was already appreciating what Hannah saw in her policeman.

"David, I'm sorry! The rice was boiling over. Happy New Year!"

"And to you, Hannah." He returned her kiss. Charlotte had gone ahead into the sitting-room.

"You've introduced yourselves?"

"After a fashion. You really landed me in it, didn't you?"

"Sorry, I couldn't resist it."

During those first minutes, as they settled in their places and drinks were poured, Webb studied Miss Yates, shocked to realize she was only slightly older than himself. Her hair, paler than Hannah's tawny mane, lay softly across her forehead, as yet untouched by grey. She had Hannah's wide grey eyes, but

36

their expression was different, and her mouth looked capable of ruthlessness. Here, he decided, was a woman of strong opinions, who could be dominating and who didn't suffer fools gladly. But she was obviously capable of great charm. Her only piece of jewellery was a heavy jade pendant on a gold chain. Some aunt! he reflected feelingly.

Charlotte in turn was engaged in her own scrutiny, and liked what she saw: the steady eyes still lit with self-mockery, the smile which transformed a hard mouth, the large policeman's hands clamped round the delicate glass. He was older than she'd expected—mid-forties, at a guess, but his brown hair was plentiful and his body lean and youthful. They were lovers, of course. She'd no doubts on that score. Yet Hannah insisted he was his own man. Having met him, she could understand that.

"I believe you live in Oxford, Miss Yates?"

"Yes, I have a little mews house near the centre."

"With a cobbled courtyard in front and a walled garden behind," Hannah elaborated. "Both pocket-size. It's idyllic, and within walking distance of practically everywhere."

"It suits me, certainly. I'd stagnate if I weren't in the centre of things."

He could believe that. "You've a lot of hobbies, I suppose?"

"If you mean interests, practically everything: music, art, history, criminology." She laughed. "I thought that might surprise you. I'm a complete amateur, of course, but the subject fascinates me. What is the mysterious something that makes one man a murderer and another, his brother even, incapable of the act?"

"It doesn't exist." Webb smiled at her raised eyebrows. "Given the circumstances, we could all commit murder, and it's those circumstances, personal to each one of us, that the police have to ferret out. Because it's they that make up the motive."

"You mean revenge, jealousy and so on? Which do you find the most common?"

"Oddly enough, one you didn't mention. Fear."

"Fear," Charlotte repeated thoughtfully. "How interesting. And there are so many different kinds."

Hannah, who had slipped out of the room during the discussion, reappeared to announce supper and the conversation dropped.

Over the meal, it turned to art and to Webb's discomfort, Hannah told her aunt of his own efforts. "He even uses his cartoons to solve his cases!" she finished.

"Does it work?" Charlotte inquired with interest.

"Quite often, yes. I find it focuses attention on a trait you may only have noted subconsciously, but which stands out in caricature. People's actions are in their faces, if you know how to read them."

"An alarming thought! Historically, of course, cartoons are invaluable as a mirror of the times. I've a prized collection of pre-war *Punches* I never tire of looking through."

"I'm afraid I'm hardly in that class!" Webb said with a smile.

"All the same," Hannah put in loyally, "the *Broadshire News* publish all they can get."

They sat at the table until it was late.

39

The warmth of the room, the good food and stimulating company produced a euphoric sense of wellbeing. Charlotte Yates intrigued Webb, intellectually rather than physically, though he found her attractive. Was this Hannah in twenty years?

Though she'd not retired with cocoa—he smiled at the thought—she did rise to her feet as the mantel clock chimed midnight.

"If you'll excuse me, I need my beauty sleep. I'm meeting a friend in Oxford for lunch, so I must be up early." She held out her hand as Webb too stood up. "I'm so glad to have met you, Chief Inspector, and I'll certainly keep an eye open for your drawings. No, don't disturb yourself, dear—" as Hannah pushed back her chair —"I have everything I need."

Webb's eyes followed her as she left the room and when he turned back to Hannah, he found her watching him. "Well, what do you think of my maiden aunt?"

"A charming lady, but one I shouldn't care to cross."

"An acute judgement." Her expression

softened. "Poor David, you look tired. Come through and relax for a while."

The sitting-room was softly lit, and a bowl of hyacinths, ramrod-stiff heralds of spring, drenched the air with their fragrance. He turned to Hannah and she moved into his arms. God, what did she see in him? A hard-bitten, disillusioned cop, divorced and with the stated intent of remaining so. Once when, stumblingly, he'd tried to explain, she had silenced him with a finger on his lips. "I'm perfectly happy with the arrangement," she'd told him. "Don't analyse it, just enjoy it."

And he did, heaven knew. He wished they could make love, but Miss Yates was awake and her presence inhibited him.

"David, if you'd like—"

"No, love. I'm sure your aunt's a broad-minded lady, but I've no intention of embarrassing either her or you. I'll sleep in my own bed tonight."

He kissed her again, still marvelling that she was happy to give and take on the same terms as himself. Then, before his resolve could weaken, he left.

Back in his own flat, the clock confirmed the passing of New Year's Day.

The new year, without capitals, was already under way. With a sense of relief, he extracted the odd sprigs of holly from behind the pictures and dropped them in the bin. Christmas decorations depressed him after the event.

Whistling softly under his breath, he prepared for bed.

3

IT was dark, rain slanted down, and the road gleamed like polished jet. The strong wind which had been around all week buffeted the car and made the writhing shadows of the trees judder crazily in the light of the street lamps. A lorry, overtaking them, sent a shower of mud across their windscreen and Sergeant Jackson swore under his breath.

Webb said, "Who found her?"

"Chap walking a dog. Ran all the way home and phoned Chedbury."

Webb pulled down his mouth. "So much for the hope of an early night. What action's been taken?"

"Doc Pringle's on his way and they've contacted Stapleton, but it'll take him a while to get there. The area's been isolated, though there won't be sightseers on a night like this. PC Linton's picking up the witness, to direct him to the scene."

"Any details on the body?"

"No, the bloke didn't look too closely. Can't say I blame him." A flurry of rain spattered against the window. "Just the weather for creeping in the undergrowth," he added gloomily.

Webb didn't reply. He could remember, not so long ago, when Chedbury was a proper village, but now ribbon development had made it little more than a suburb of Shillingham. However, the countryside lay just beyond, and Chedbury Woods was a well-known beauty spot. Though why anyone should walk his dog there in belting rain at ten o'clock on a January evening, Webb couldn't imagine.

They had come through the village and Jackson turned to the left down a bumpy unmade road which led to the woods. Ahead of them, a couple of cars were parked so that their headlights illumined as much as possible of the grass and undergrowth by the side of the road. As they drew in behind, a cloaked and helmeted figure emerged from the shadows and bent to the window.

"'Evening, sir. PC Linton, Chedbury. I've got the witness in my car, sir. Doctor Pringle's with the body now."

44

"Scenes of Crime not here?"

"Not yet, sir."

Webb turned up the collar of his coat and climbed out of the car. The icy rain blew in his face, momentarily taking his breath.

"She wasn't right in the woods, then?"

"No, sir, just on the edge, under some bushes. It was the dog sniffed her out, Mr. Beddows says."

Webb opened the door of the Panda car and leant inside. In the passenger seat a man was sitting huddled in a raincoat, rubbing his hands for warmth. "Good evening, sir. Mr. Beddows? Chief Inspector Webb, Shillingham CID. When I've had a word with the doctor, I'll be back for a preliminary statement."

The man nodded miserably. No doubt he was wishing he'd kept the dog on a leash, taken another direction—anything, rather than the sequence of events that had led to his present situation.

Dr. Pringle, tall and unfailingly cheerful whatever the circumstances, was picking his way back to the car. "Good evening, Chief Inspector. Well, she's dead, all right. Has been for some time, by the look

45

of her. The body's cold and rigor mortis is starting to wear off."

"Which would make it—what?—twenty-four hours ago?"

"Roughly. Didn't move her, of course. She's lying face down, with her head to one side."

"Cause of death?"

"Looks like strangulation." They turned as fresh headlights raked over them. Another car had left the main road and was bumping along towards them. "Here comes the Scenes of Crime boys. The sooner they can get a tent up, the easier for all concerned."

Webb said, "Perhaps you'd take a look at the witness, Doc. Confirm he's fit to make a statement, and so on."

The three men who were climbing out of the last car wore heavy boots and plastic raincapes. One had a camera, another stakes and rope, and the third began to unload arc lamps from the boot. PC Linton re-emerged from the shadows.

"I used tape to mark the route, sir, and weighted it with stones. It was the way Mr. Beddows took in the first place—the grass was flattened."

"Thank you, Constable. I'll have a quick look myself, before the boys get busy. You stay here, Jackson. We want the minimum of traffic till the scene's been examined."

The tape line gleamed faintly in the light of his torch. Keeping to it, Webb made his way through the long, drenched grass to a clump of gorse bushes. Behind them, and just on the fringe of the woods, lay the woman's body.

His first reaction was surprise, though there was no logic in it. This was a very smart corpse. Her fur jacket, even in such adverse conditions, was recognizably genuine, and the heavy tweed of her skirt looked good quality. She was also wearing gloves. A pity: there'd be nothing useful under the nails, and no betraying scratches on her killer.

Impossible, at this first inspection, to judge her age. The grotesque death-mask, with the tongue forced out of the mouth, distorted the face sufficiently to preclude any guesswork.

Webb pulled out his pocket book and, awkwardly balancing the torch, made a quick sketch of the position of the body.

Then, turning carefully within the compass of his footsteps, he walked back the way he had come. "OK," he said to the huddle of waiting men. "She's all yours."

"Any leads, Guv?"

Jackson's sandy hair was plastered against his head and the rain dripped steadily off his craggy eyebrows. But beneath them, the china-blue eyes were bright with interest.

"Give us a chance, Ken!"

"The Support Group are here. They've started searching along the road."

"Right. Get through to Inspector Crombie and ask him to stand by to interview Mr. Beddows. We'll have to wait here till the lads have finished."

Smoothing his hands over his hair to remove the rain, Webb climbed into the Chedbury police car.

"Now, Mr. Beddows, sorry to keep you waiting. Can I have your full name and address, please?"

"Frank Arthur Beddows, Three, Meadow End, Chedbury."

"Is that this end of the village?"

"That's right. Last turn-off on the left. Coming from Shillingham, that is."

"Do you always walk your dog this time of night?"

"Regular as clockwork. When the news finishes, he runs to fetch his lead."

"Hail, rain or snow?"

Beddows grimaced. "There's no arguing with him. If it's really bad we just go round the block."

"But not tonight?"

"Wish to God I had, I can tell you. Point was, me and the wife had had words. I wanted to get out for a bit."

"You left at the usual time?"

"A little before. Nine-fifteen or so. It wasn't too bad then, just a drizzle. I hardly noticed it."

"Do you take the same route every evening?"

"Oh no. I only come this far in the summer, when it's light longer. But tonight I was in no hurry to get home."

"So you didn't come along here last night, for instance?"

Beddows frowned, turning sideways to look at Webb. "What's last night got to do with it?"

49

"Just answer the question, please, Mr. Beddows. What route did you take last night?"

"Through the village and over the bridge." His tone was surly at the implied rebuke.

"In the opposite direction, in fact?"

"Yes."

Too bad the row hadn't been twenty-four hours earlier.

"Right, to get back to tonight, then. Once off the main road, you let the dog loose?"

"That's it. He likes to run ahead."

"And how exactly did you find the body?"

The man shuddered. "Well, as I said, Scamp shot off, and almost at once I was sorry I'd let him. The rain was starting in earnest and I was in two minds about turning back."

"Go on."

"Then I heard him barking, didn't I? Couldn't see a thing, of course. Called to him, but he wouldn't come, and that's not like him. Went on barking like mad, and it wasn't his usual bark, neither. I thought he'd got a rabbit, and I didn't want to leave it half-dead or anything. I could just make him out in the bushes—there's a lot of white on him—and I made my way over, getting soaked in the process." Beddows' voice shook. "Well, I—I could see something there, just a bit darker than the ground. I bent down and felt around." He broke off, fists clenched on his knees.

"What part of the body did you touch?" Webb's voice was carefully neutral.

"Her leg. God, I wouldn't like to live through that again. I spoke to her. Sounds stupid, doesn't it, but I thought she might just be hurt or asleep. Said something daft like, 'Are you all right?' But I knew really. She was so cold and—and stiff, and it stood to reason no one'd be lying there from choice. I grabbed hold of Scamp. My hands were shaking and I couldn't manage the clasp, so I threaded the lead through his collar and we ran like hell all the way home."

"And phoned the station as soon as you got in?"

"When I'd got my breath back and told the wife. And I thought that was the end of it," he added truculently. "Didn't expect to be dragged back here and kept up half the night answering questions. I'm not a bloody criminal, you know."

"No one thinks you are, Mr. Beddows." As yet. "But whoever finds a body is crucial to the investigation. Odd things you noticed or suddenly remember could be vital. Which is why I've asked one of my officers to take you to Shillingham to make a full statement."

"Now?" Beddows's voice rose. "It's gone eleven."

"I know, I'm sorry. We won't keep you any longer than necessary. If your wife will be worrying, you can phone her when you get there."

He got out before Beddows could protest further. "Ken, get the Support car to run our friend to Carrington Street."

He opened the passenger door and handed Beddows over to Jackson, watching as the man reluctantly climbed inside the last car in line. And as the driver reversed and started back towards the road, another car turned into it. The pathologist had arrived. The murder team was complete.

Twelve hours later, Webb reached his

office and slumped into his chair. "Coffee, for the love of Allah!"

Inspector Crombie grinned. "Been at the PM?"

"Yep. Not one of my favourite pastimes."

"And what did they find?"

"The only new fact was bruising on the left side of the face, hidden when she was lying down. Must have been caused before death, not as the body hit the ground. As regards time, body-cooling's slowed down by asphyxiation but since the process had finished anyway and rigor mortis was wearing off, we'll have to rely on stomach contents. They show she'd had a light meal four hours or so before death. Lunch, most likely, say between twelve and two."

"So she died roughly between four and six on Wednesday?"

Webb nodded his thanks as a typist, after a brief knock, came in with a cup of coffee.

"As near as we can tell. She was wearing an expensive watch, bracelet and wedding ring and her handbag was underneath the body. About fifty pounds in the purse, so robbery wasn't the motive. Her bag contained the usual things." He consulted a piece of paper. "Car keys—could be a lead there—compact, a bunch of house keys, lipstick, comb, etcetera. But no cheque-book and no credit cards. She mightn't have needed them if she'd enough cash; on the other hand, they could have been removed to delay identification."

"Sexual assault?"

"No. Surprising, in the circumstances."

"And she was dumped after death?"

"She'd have to be, wouldn't she? A well-dressed, well-heeled woman like that wouldn't be rambling in the woods. I've asked for the missing persons files. We'll see if any of them fit."

"So what's the description?"

"Late thirties/early forties, height five foot two, weight eight stone. Brown curly hair, brown eyes. Appendix scar. No dentures, but some extensive bridgework. A chart's being circulated. Her clothes have gone to the lab but they're all quality stuff. Squirrel-fur jacket, cashmere jumper, silk underwear, lizardskin shoes and bag. Not, you'd think, a nobody who could disappear without someone getting steamed up about it."

But half an hour later, after a painstaking search through the files, it seemed the dead woman had not been missed. No one listed bore any resemblance to her.

"The *Broadshire News* have been on," Crombie said. "We could ask their help."

"Yes, phone Romilly. Get him to put a full description on the front page—both the *Evening News* and tomorrow's *Weekly*. That may bring someone forward. What did you think of Beddows?"

"I doubt if he knows more than he says."

"Sorry I didn't manage to look in. By the time I'd finished it was around one. He waited till the statement was typed?"

"With bad grace, yes." Crombie grinned. "Well, he said he wasn't in a hurry to get home!"

"Four hours previously! I reckon a minor squabble would be forgotten when he did arrive. More important things to talk about. So, what have we got? Probably dumped after death but no drag marks, so her killer must have carried her. No problem there, she was small and light.

He probably parked where we did. Then he tossed her handbag down and dropped her on top of it, partially concealed by the gorse bush. It was his bad luck Beddows and the dog came along. At this time of year, she could have lain for weeks without being discovered."

"No identifying tyre marks, I suppose?"

"After half a dozen police cars? Even without them it was a non-starter, with all that rain. We've got house-to-house under way in Chedbury, but damn it, the village is on the main road. No one's likely to notice one car unless they saw it turn off towards the woods. That's what we're hoping for, but I'm not holding my breath."

The Inspector pushed back his chair and went to the map on the wall. "I wonder where she came from. The killer wouldn't drive further than he need. A dead body's not the most comfortable of cargoes."

"That applies to where she was killed, not where she lived. She could have come from anywhere. God, Alan, what a start to the new year! January not a week old, and we've a murder on our hands."

"Will you be working from Chedbury?"

"Not worth it. Apart from being found there, I doubt if she'd any connection with it, and we can be there in ten minutes if required. I'm going back now, actually. Want to have a look round in daylight. Scenes of Crime are still there: they did the essentials last night, then packed in until it got light. Let's hope they've got some lead on who she was."

Minutes later, Webb and Jackson were retracing their journey of the previous night. The rain had finished, the sun was shining, and everything looked fresh. With a less jaundiced eye, Webb conceded that Chedbury was still a pretty village. Unlike many others, it had achieved a happy amalgam of old and new, the modern cottages in honey-coloured stone fitting companionably between their thatched neighbours. The central square boasted a clock tower and round this, stalls precariously balanced on the cobblestones, the Friday market was now in progress.

Jackson slowed to a crawl to avoid the crowds spilling off the pavements, and as they negotiated a succession of barrows, pushchairs and bicycles, Webb had ample time to observe Meadow End on their left.

By now, Frank Beddows would be at work in the Shillingham supermarket. Webb could imagine him the centre of attention as he related his gruesome findings of the night before.

A uniformed policeman, recognizing the car, touched his helmet as Jackson turned down the rough road, its surface churned by the unaccustomed traffic. A small knot of people stood at the junction, staring across the fields to the hive of activity on the fringe of the wood. Webb could see screens flapping and several parked cars.

"Nothing fresh, Guv," the senior Scenes of Crime man greeted him. "We've been over it with a fine-tooth comb. No hope of a cast of footprints. They wouldn't show on grass, quite apart from Beddows's prints and our own. There were traces of blood where the victim's head lay—probably from the bitten tongue. We've covered a wide area round about, but for my money he parked where we did, dumped her, and drove off again. It'll be the hell of a job to track him down. Her wearing gloves was sheer bad luck."

"No helpful diary fell out of her handbag?"

58

Hodges grinned. "Afraid not. Any luck on the car keys?"

"They're being gone over now."

With Jackson following them, the two men walked over the crushed grass to the tent. Webb lifted the flap and went in, nodding to the man who, on hands and knees, was collecting samples from the indented area where the victim had lain. Out of the wind and with the sun shining on the polythene, the tent was claustrophobically warm. Webb felt the sweat start in his armpits.

He turned and emerged. Hodges and Jackson, hands in pockets, were staring with narrowed eyes along the road. He followed the direction of their gaze. "Can you get back to the main road along there, or would he have to double back?"

"That's what we're wondering, Guv. Shall we see where it goes?"

"Might as well. Not much we can do here. Thanks, Dick. Look forward to the report in due course."

Webb and Jackson returned to their car, but before getting in Webb walked ahead a short distance, staring intently at the surface of the road.

"Damn!" he said under his breath, then raised his voice. "Dick, get your lads to look along the road a bit. None of our cars went beyond here. You might find a tyre imprint, though by the look of it some ruddy great tractor's been along and made a thorough job of destroying any evidence."

Hodges came up and peered at the road. "Will do, but I think you're right."

"Could they have a go now? I'd like to drive along, but I don't want to obliterate anything."

He leant against the car, watching as they painstakingly searched the road, camera at the ready. A hundred yards along, the surface changed to a cinder track and Hodges came back, shaking his head.

"We've snapped what there is, but I'm not hopeful. All we can see is the tractor tread, and even that disappears on the cinders."

"Right. We'll go along then, and see where we come out."

They did not have to go far. After a few hundred yards, the cinder track curved round and ended at a farm gateway. Beyond it, in the yard, stood the tractor.

"Drive in, Ken," Webb instructed. "Might as well have a word while we're here."

At the sound of their car, the farmer appeared round the side of a barn.

"Good morning, sir. Webb, Shillingham CID."

"Ah. Saw your men along the track. Trouble, is there?"

"I'm afraid so. A woman's body has been found. Did you happen to see or hear anything suspicious on Wednesday evening?"

The man thought for a moment, scratching his ear. "Can't say I did. Didn't go down that way at all Wednesday. We was working the fields back of the house."

"But the tractor's been along recently?"

"Yesterday morn, that were. Didn't see nothing, but wasn't looking, mind."

"You didn't by any chance hear a car drive up, perhaps hoping to find his way back to the main road?"

"What time would that be, then?"

"Probably—between five and seven."

"Nah. After the milking we shut up for the night and stopped indoors."

"Well, if you remember anything, we'd be glad to hear from you."

The farmer nodded and stood watching, his dog at his heels, as Jackson reversed and they drove back through the gate.

"So the question now," Jackson said, "is did he turn left at the main road, or drive back through Chedbury?"

"*Back*, Ken? We don't know he came that way."

"If he came from the other direction, the nearest village is Chipping Claydon, fifteen miles away. There are plenty of woods and bushes along the road: why drive this far with her?"

"You've got a point there. Of course, he could have killed her in the car, only seconds before he dumped her."

They were approaching the police cars again, and Inspector Hodges stood at the roadside with one of his officers.

"Slow down a minute, Ken." Webb wound down his window and the Inspector came over. "No joy along there, Dick. It's a dead end round that bend, a farmyard.

They didn't see or hear a thing. We're on our own, I'm afraid."

The car moved on. "Was it manual strangulation, Guv?" Jackson asked suddenly.

"Yes, the PM confirmed that. Why?"

The Sergeant grinned, his blue eyes twinkling. "At least when we find the murder weapon, we'll also have the bloke that did it!"

They were coming into the village again. "Reckon friend Beddows comes back for lunch?" Webb inquired.

"Might do. He's near enough."

"Let's drop in then, since we're almost passing his door. Number three, Meadow End—first on your right."

It was a short road of semi-detached houses, and No. 3 was on the left. There was no car in the driveway, but Webb nodded to Jackson and the two men got out and walked up the path.

Their ring was answered by a small dark woman with a pointed nose and thin mouth. Jackson could understand Beddows keeping out of her way.

"Yes?"

"Good afternoon, Mrs. Beddows. I'm Webb and this is Sergeant Jackson."

The mouth tightened still more. "Yes?"

"Is your husband home, by any chance?"

"No, he isn't. He's at work. Had to get up as usual, though he didn't get much sleep, and no more did I." She stared at him accusingly.

"We thought," Webb said placatingly, "that he might come home for lunch."

"Oh, I couldn't be doing with that. It's bad enough having to cook for the kids. I told him straight, once they go to secondary it'll be school dinners regardless of the cost. I've earned a bit of time to myself."

"I'm sure you have, yes."

She folded her arms, determined not to ask them inside. The wind was still strong, blowing the flaps of their mackintoshes as they stood there. There'd be small comfort in this house, Jackson thought, feeling a rush of warmth for his own placid Millie.

"If that's all, then—?"

"Yes, there's nothing important. I wanted to thank your husband for his

64

help, and apologize for not seeing him before he left the station."

"He got over it."

There was a crash from the kitchen, followed by a scream and some high-pitched yelling.

"There! That's what happens when I turn my back." Wasting no more time on the policemen, Mrs. Beddows slammed the door. Behind its thin wood, they could hear her raised voice as she shouted at the children.

"Wedded bliss!" said Jackson.

Webb grunted, turning back down the path, and the Sergeant regretted his remark. The Governor's marriage had ended in divorce. It didn't do to be flippant. To change the subject, and at the same time introduce one close to his heart, he said casually, "Nice little pub they've got here. Happened to notice, as we came through."

Webb grinned. "Pint of bitter and a plateful of cottage pie? Why not? And who knows, by the time we get back, we might have a positive ID."

65

4

"CHIEF INSPECTOR WEBB? Sergeant Fenton, sir, on the desk. Gentleman here worried about his wife. She didn't show up when expected."

Webb straightened, suddenly alert. "Thank you, Fenton. Tell him I'll be right down." He replaced the receiver and looked at Crombie. "Bloke looking for his wife. Perhaps things are moving at last."

"Want me to make myself scarce?"

"If you wouldn't mind, Alan. I'll need Ken here, and we don't want to crowd him."

He ran down the stairs and the man at the duty desk turned to face him. Webb assessed him rapidly: late forties, thick red-brown hair, deep-set grey eyes and a bump on the bridge of his nose.

He went forward and introduced himself. The man took his outstretched hand.

"Oliver Pendrick. I've come for some advice, actually."

66

"I see, sir. If you'll come up to my office—?"

Webb led the way upstairs, slightly puzzled. Advice? The man certainly wasn't frantic, yet their victim had been dead three days. Perhaps after all this was a different matter.

"Sergeant Jackson, Mr. Pendrick. Now, perhaps you'll sit down and tell us what we can do for you."

Pendrick took the proffered chair and crossed his legs, completely at ease. There was an air of authority about him which suggested he was more used to conducting interviews than being subjected to them. Perhaps in his view he was conducting this one.

"It's a little embarrassing, really, which is why I preferred to explain in person rather than on the phone. The point is my wife's been in London all week and was due home last night. She didn't arrive, and there's been no word from her. I was particularly annoyed as we were dining with friends."

Annoyed, not worried. "You had to cancel it?"

Oliver Pendrick shifted in his chair.

67

"Well, no. I went alone." Webb made no comment, but he apparently felt the need for an explanation. "For one thing, it was very short notice, and for another—well, unfortunately my wife and I didn't part on the best of terms, and I felt she was trying to embarrass me."

"What did you tell your hosts?"

"That she'd been delayed but would try to get along later. Actually, that's what I thought would happen. When she didn't come, I was sure I'd find her at home."

"But there was no sign of her?"

"No. So this morning I phoned her London flat, but she wasn't there either. I was a little concerned, and wondered if I should contact the police in London. That's what I wanted to ask you."

"You're afraid something might have happened to her?"

"Not really; Nancy's more than capable of looking after herself. But it's unlike her not to be in touch if she's changed her plans. She runs a catering company, but as they're not open on Saturdays and I don't know the staff's private numbers, that's no help. I'm probably wasting your time; she might well have arrived by now."

"Could you give me a description of your wife, sir?"

Pencil poised, Sergeant Jackson held his breath.

"She's small, slim build, curly brown hair. That's about all."

"And what makes you sure she's in London?"

Pendrick looked at him in surprise. "Because she was hell-bent on getting back there; that was the cause of the unpleasantness. We had guests in the house, and I thought it discourteous as well as unnecessary to insist on leaving."

"So when was the last time you saw her?"

"First thing on Tuesday morning. I own The Gables Hotel in Frecklemarsh. I went over there just before eight, and Nancy was on the point of leaving then."

The telephone interrupted him. Murmuring an apology, Webb reached for it.

"Alan here, Guv. Thought you'd like to know we've traced the Scirocco that was towed in yesterday. Belongs to a Mrs.

Nancy Pendrick, Six Belsize Gardens, NW3. And guess what? The keys from the handbag fit it a treat."

"Thank you, Inspector. Where and when was it left?"

"Duke Street multi-storey, Wednesday p.m. Clocked in at sixteen hundred on the nail."

Webb put the phone down and turned back to Pendrick. "Your wife was leaving the house when you last saw her. I presume she was travelling by car?"

"Of course."

"Is it possible she didn't after all go to London?"

Pendrick frowned impatiently. "No, Chief Inspector, it is not. As I've explained, that was the whole point of her leaving. In any case, she forwarded a bill to me. It had a London postmark."

Webb leant forward. "When did you receive it, sir?"

"Yesterday."

"Did you notice the postmark?"

"No, I didn't, but since it came second-class, it was probably Wednesday."

"Have you still got the envelope?"

"Look, what is this? What does it

matter when it was posted? Nancy was in London all right, and in all probability still is. Where else is she likely to be?"

His question hung on the air. Very slowly he straightened and uncrossed his legs. "What is it, Chief Inspector? You're leading up to something. Do you know where she is?"

"I'm afraid I might, sir. Have you seen a newspaper in the last couple of days?"

"I've not had time. Why?"

"A woman's body was found on Thursday, by Chedbury Woods. She—"

"You're suggesting it could be *Nancy*? But that's ridiculous! She's never been to Chedbury in her life."

Just in her death, Webb thought grimly. He was no longer in doubt. "Sir, I think I should warn you—"

"Look, *if* Nancy came rushing back to Broadshire, which I don't believe for a minute, why on earth should she go to Chedbury? Her only friends in the county are in Frecklemarsh, and to be honest they're my friends rather than hers. I should explain she's my second wife. We've only been married three years."

"Sir, I'm very sorry, and I hope I'm

71

wrong, but I think it would be advisable for you to—take a look at the body."

Pendrick stared at him, and the colour left his face. He said slowly, "My God, you're serious, aren't you? You really think it's Nancy you've got down there. But it *can't* be. She's in London—unless she's home by now." He glanced a little wildly at the phone. The Chief Inspector rose to his feet.

"It'll only take a minute, sir."

Shillingham town centre was allegedly planned by a policeman with a wooden leg. All relevant buildings were conveniently close together and, as often before, Webb was grateful that the hospital and mortuary were next to the police station. He wondered if he'd ever be able to watch dispassionately when the long drawer was pulled out and the sheet folded back from the dead face. For a full two minutes Oliver Pendrick stood rigid, staring down. It was as well they'd prettied the poor woman up a bit. Then he turned, met Webb's eyes and gave a brief nod.

Webb put a hand under his elbow and led him back to the station. Jackson had some tea ready. Automatically, Pendrick lifted the nearest cup and drank. If it burned his mouth, he gave no sign. He spoke for the first time since seeing his wife's body.

"I presume it was a traffic accident?"

"I'm afraid not, Mr. Pendrick. Your wife was strangled."

There was a silence, then Pendrick said hoarsely, "Is this some kind of joke?"

"No, sir. Her body was found on Thursday night, but she'd been there since the previous evening."

"But who—I mean, why—? I don't understand. How can Nancy, who was alive on Wednesday morning in London, be dead on Wednesday evening in Chedbury?"

"That's something we'll have to find out, sir. I'm afraid there are some questions I'll have to ask, but if you'd rather we left it for a while—"

"Let's get it over, for God's sake. I'll tell you all I know, but it won't be much help."

"We'll start with the formalities, then."

Methodically, Jackson took them down: Pendrick's full name and address and that of his wife, the details of their oddly split life. No, she'd no children by either marriage. Yes, he had two: their names and ages.

"Who else was in the house last weekend?"

"My brother-in-law and his wife were staying a few days."

"Your wife's brother?"

"My first wife's. And we had a party on Saturday, New Year's Eve." He paused, added wonderingly, "Only a week ago."

"Was it a large party, sir?"

"Not more than twenty, counting ourselves."

"I'll need the names and addresses later. And you say, sir, you and your wife had a disagreement?"

Briefly Pendrick put a hand across his eyes. "Yes. I can't change it now, but I'm sorry we parted like that."

"Was it serious?"

"Not really. I was annoyed about her spending so little time with us. She retaliated by saying I neglected my family."

"Which you resented."

"Of course. Admittedly the hotel takes up a lot of my time; that's only to be expected; but Henry and Rose aren't children any longer."

"Perhaps they need more, rather than less, of your time now?"

It was an astute remark from a man with no children. Pendrick resented it, though he made no reply. He probably thought Webb spoke from experience.

"Are your brother-and-sister-in-law still with you, Mr. Pendrick?"

"No, they went home on Thursday."

"And they are—?"

"Mr. and the Honourable Mrs. Roger Beresford, Heron Court, Chardsey, Surrey. They've a London flat too."

Webb looked up. "Would that be the barrister?"

"Correct."

"A brilliant man. I always follow his cases."

The questions went on, and the Pendricks' home life began to emerge. Oliver admitted frankly that his children hadn't accepted his second wife. "Though things might have been improving," he added. "Nancy said Henry'd gone to her with a problem."

"Do you know what it was?"

"No idea. He leapt up at that point and said it was confidential."

"And that was last weekend?"

"Yes."

"Might he have been in the habit of turning to her?"

"I doubt it. Nancy wouldn't have missed the chance to tell me." He paused. "I shouldn't have said that. I don't want to give the impression we were always quarrelling. We had our good times, too."

"I'm sure you did, sir," Webb said smoothly. "Now, will you tell me, please, where you were between four and six on Wednesday afternoon?"

Pendrick stared at him, a pulse beating in his temple. He moistened his lips. "At the hotel. I had some paperwork to see to."

"And the other members of the household?"

"My son was in the hotel kitchens; he's learning the business. I don't know about Rose, but my sister-in-law had a hair appointment. Her husband drove her to Shillingham, which is why I felt free to work."

"What time did they return?"

"I don't know. I was on duty that evening, and didn't get back till late." His thoughts moved on. "There's so much I don't understand. Nancy's car, for instance. Is it missing, or was it found near her?"

"It was left in the car park in Duke Street."

"Then how did she get to Chedbury? None of it makes sense. And if she was as near home as that, why didn't she contact us?"

"Did she know anyone who lived in Shillingham?"

"Not a soul."

"Might she perhaps have arranged at the party to meet someone?"

"If she had, she wouldn't have gone back to London."

"Unless she'd an important engagement?"

Pendrick shrugged. "I've no idea what she does up there. She runs a cookery school and a catering firm, but she never discusses them with me, nor what she does in her spare time."

"You don't know if she'd any gentlemen friends?"

77

"Lovers, you mean? I doubt it. Nancy met men on her own terms, but she wasn't dependent on them. Sex was something she could take or leave."

"Was your own relationship satisfactory?"

Pendrick looked up, an angry flush staining his cheeks, then the fire went out of him. "I suppose you have to ask. It was all right, but not like it had been with Avis."

"Your first wife?" Webb paused. He'd have to go into that marriage too, see if there were any links that could be relevant, but not yet. They'd enough to occupy them for the moment.

Pendrick said awkwardly, "Why did you ask about men? I mean, she hadn't—?"

"There was no sign of recent intercourse, either before or after death."

"Thank you." He spoke with dignity, and Jackson cleared his throat. Poor bugger, he thought. "Presumably," Pendrick added, "that means there's been a post mortem?"

"Yes, and the inquest's on Monday, at four-thirty." Webb studied his face. It was just beginning to sink in, he thought, unless this is all one big act, which had been known to happen. In the meantime, he'd better press on.

"Did your wife have any connection with the staff or guests at the hotel?"

"No, she—my God!" Pendrick stared at him and he waited patiently. "I've just remembered something, though I doubt if it's important. Her ex-husband was working at the hotel until six weeks ago."

Webb laid down his pen. "She was aware of that?"

"She found out the same time I did."

"Then you hadn't engaged him?"

"No, the head barman hires the bar staff. At least no one at the hotel knew who he was."

"How long had he been there when you found out?"

"A month or so. I'd seen him around, but I hadn't heard his surname. Even if I had, I doubt if it'd have registered. He was the last person I'd expect to see behind my own bar."

"So what happened?"

"Nancy arrived one Friday, and since no one was home, she came over to the hotel. I met her in the hall and we went to the bar, where Dean was on duty. She just stopped and stared at him. He smiled sheepishly and said, 'Hello, Nance.' And she burst out laughing. I'd no idea what was going on."

"And you fired him?"

"I suggested it, but she said no. She told me he never kept a job for long, so it might as well run its course. I remember her saying, 'You have to hand it to him, don't you?'"

"And eventually, as she predicted, he left of his own accord?"

Pendrick smiled grimly. "Not quite. He was found with his fingers in the till."

"When was that?"

"Some time in November."

"And where did he go then, do you know?"

"Back to London, I suppose. He's a Londoner through and through."

"Did he explain why he'd come to your hotel?"

"Some cliché about seeing how the other half live."

"And until your wife walked into the bar he'd made no attempt to contact her?"

"Apparently not."

"And afterwards?"

"He touched her for money once or twice. I was very annoyed, but as she didn't hesitate to point out, it was her money and there was nothing I could do about it."

Webb doodled thoughtfully on his pad. "What kind of man is Dean?"

"The kind that appeals to women. Handsome, plausible and weak. He always lands on his feet, because there's always some woman who'll take pity on him."

"Would he have left a forwarding address?"

"Possibly, when he realized we weren't going to prosecute. I can find out."

"I'm afraid, Mr. Pendrick, we'll have to see the staff, whether they knew your wife or not. And your family, of course."

"My family? Why?"

"There might be some light they can throw on why she was in the district."

"I very much doubt it. She wouldn't confide in Rose or Henry."

"Even so, they'll have to be questioned, but we won't intrude until—"

"If it's got to be done, there's no point

in delaying it. Come back with me now, if you like. Nancy wasn't their mother; they didn't even like her particularly. They'll be shocked, but certainly not heart-broken."

Webb glanced at Jackson who, behind Pendrick's back, raised his eyebrows and shrugged.

"Very well, Mr. Pendrick, if that's what you'd prefer. We'll run you back and you can leave your car here. Forensic will need to look at it, anyway. Purely routine," he added, at Pendrick's frown. "Now, who's likely to be home at the moment?"

"My son and daughter and the house-keeper. They won't be able to help, but you're welcome to question them."

"We'll also need to examine your wife's possessions, any papers and so on."

"There again, you won't find much. She kept most of her things in London."

"I'll be going there tomorrow. I imagine the keys will be among those in her handbag."

Pendrick said diffidently, "Where are her things? The ones she—had with her?"

"They've been sent to the laboratory for examination."

"I see." He was silent for a moment, then rose determinedly to his feet. "Very well, Chief Inspector, I'm ready when you are."

Avoiding each other's eyes, the three men went together out of the room.

5

FRECKLEMARSH was not one of Webb's favourite villages; it had about it a self-conscious charm that irritated him. You came upon it round a bend at the top of a hill, stretching down the gentle slope and fanning out at the foot into the main village.

In that first bird's eye view, all its salient features were visible, the river Darrant spanned by stone bridges, and over to the right the cobbled square with its cluster of specialist shops, none of which, Webb felt, had any place in a proper village—wine-store, delicatessen, craft gallery. Even the church, reputedly Norman, was too pretty for his taste, set artistically on a green mound with its marble tombstones glinting in the sun.

It was the tombstones which recalled his attention, and he glanced in the mirror at their passenger. Pendrick hadn't spoken during the fifteen-minute drive. He was staring out of the window and Webb felt a stab of sympathy. It was the hell of a thing to be faced with. Then suddenly, unaware he was watched, his mouth twisted into a smile and Webb's pity evaporated. What, in the present circumstances, could have caused him even fleeting amusement?

He said brusquely, "Once we're over the bridge you'll have to direct us, sir." His eyes were still on Pendrick, and the man started, coming back to the present.

"Keep straight on. It's about half a mile on the left." He paused. "The Gables was originally the Squire's house, some distance from the village, and the cottages where I live housed estate workers. However, a spate of building after the last war narrowed the gap, as you see."

The little speech, oddly formal, sounded like a quotation from the brochure. Neither of the policemen offered any comment.

As they passed the gate with the hotel board, Pendrick leant forward. "Here we are—on the left. You can drive in, I left the gates open." He laughed briefly. "Do you know, I found myself looking for Nancy's car. Habit, I suppose."

Webb's compassion would have been stronger had he not seen that reflected smile.

They drew up with a crunching of gravel and the three men climbed out. The driveway was at the end of the long, low house which stretched parallel to the road, the façade of the original cottages still clearly visible. The main entrance was in the end wall. Pendrick went ahead and opened the door, standing aside to let the policemen in. Webb, a diligent absorber of atmosphere, paused to assess it.

The conversion had been skilfully done. From where they stood in the small hall, they could see through a series of archways to the far end of the house, each section, no doubt, the width of an original cottage. It was very much a country home; the floor was tiled in red and in the alcove to their right an assortment of jackets and anoraks were untidily bunched on hooks. Beneath them stood some muddy boots and a bag of golf clubs. A steep flight of stairs led upwards, at the foot of which was a door which Pendrick now opened. An appetizing smell reached them, and a pleasant-faced woman turned from the stove.

"Are Henry and Rose in, Mrs. Foldes?"

"Yes, sir, in the sitting-room, I think. We were just wondering if you'd be back for lunch. There's still no word from Mrs. Nancy." She caught sight of the men behind him, and her eyes widened in alarm. "There's nothing wrong, is there, sir?"

"You'd better hear this too. Come through."

The ceiling was low, and Webb ducked as he went under the archway before realizing that Pendrick, his own height, had preceded him. They passed through the dining area, the table laid for lunch, and under the final arch. The sitting-room turned, L-shaped, to the right forming a large square, which at present was dominated by a Christmas tree. Lounging on a sofa in T-shirt and jeans was the loveliest girl Webb had seen. Her hair, a deep honey-gold, framed an oval face with sultry, long-lashed eyes of smoky grey. Come-to-bed eyes, if ever he'd seen them. He heard Jackson's indrawn breath, and grinned mentally.

There was also a young man present, who, hearing footsteps, turned from the window.

"At last!" he exclaimed. "We were just beginning to wonder—" His voice trailed off as he registered the silent group behind his father.

Pendrick plunged straight into his announcement. "These gentlemen are from the police. I'm afraid I've some bad news. Nancy's dead. She's—been murdered."

There was a moment's electric silence. Then the boy and the housekeeper exclaimed together—murmurs of conventional disbelief. But having scanned all three faces in that first second, Webb's eyes came to rest on the girl. She was pushing herself back against the sofa as though to escape from something she could not bear. Her wide, horrified eyes were fixed on her father.

"No!" she said violently. "No, no, no!"

The extent of her shock seemed unexpected, since the others turned to her. The housekeeper took a step forward. "Miss Rose—" but the girl still stared at Oliver.

"She *can't* be!" she said almost pleadingly. "It's just not possible. Oh God, God, it isn't true, is it? *Is it?*"

Her father was clearly at a loss. He said more gently, "I'm afraid so. It's hard to believe, I know. I can't imagine—"

Her tension suddenly snapped. She hurled herself sideways on the sofa, burying her face in the cushions and pounding them with her fists.

Pendrick said tersely, "Get some brandy," and went to his daughter. The boy's face was ashen, but Webb suspected that his sister's reaction had shocked him more than the death of his stepmother. Stiffly, obediently, he moved to the drinks tray.

Mrs. Foldes had started to tremble. "Oh, the poor lady!" she murmured, and, suddenly connecting facts, looked up at Webb. "That lady in the paper, sir. Was *that* Mrs. Nancy?"

He nodded.

"But we thought she was in London."

Pendrick raised his daughter's shoulders and pulled her against him. "Darling, I'm sorry. I didn't think you'd be so upset."

She made no sound, but tears streamed from her eyes. Like a docile child, she sipped from the glass he held, shuddering as she swallowed the liquid. In the pallor of her face, her eyes had darkened to slate and Webb could see fear in them.

"Have they got him?" she whispered.

"Got who, love?"

She checked herself, swallowed, drew a breath. "The—the man who did it."

"Not yet, but they will. That's why these gentlemen are here. They want to ask us—"

Rose said in a high voice, "I don't know *anything*—anything at all." Pushing her father aside, she came suddenly to her feet and, brushing past the group in the archway, ran stumblingly from the room. There was a brief silence. Henry still stood in the middle of the room, an expression of disbelief on his face. Either Pendrick had underestimated his children's affections, or there was some other cause for their distress. They must be questioned before they'd a chance to confer.

"Lord save us—my pie!" Mrs. Foldes hurried back to the kitchen. Webb said quietly, "We'll disturb you as little as possible, Mr. Pendrick, and I know your meal is ready, but if we could just have a word with your son here?"

A look of alarm crossed the boy's face and Jackson thought he'd repeat his sister's disclaimer. But Pendrick was saying heavily, "Yes, of course, I'll leave you to it. And you'll need to eat yourselves. I'll ask Mrs. Foldes to prepare something."

Left with the police, Henry Pendrick licked his lips nervously. "I'm afraid I shan't be much help. I didn't even know Nancy was in Broadshire. She was due last night, but she never turned up." He paused, then added, "Well, of course she didn't."

Webb moved into the room and sat down, motioning Jackson to do likewise. "When did you last see her, Mr. Pendrick?"

"Monday evening. We were all in here —my uncle and aunt as well, watching TV. Rose and I sat up for the late film and the others went to bed."

"You didn't see her the following morning?"

"No, she'd gone by the time I got up."

"How did she seem on Monday? Was

she relaxed, or could she have been worried about something?"

"She was—the same as usual."

"Did you get on well with her?"

"Not particularly."

"Why was that?"

"She got our backs up when she first came. Tried to boss us around, and so on."

"But that was three years ago. Hadn't things improved since?"

"Not really."

Yet according to his father, Henry had gone to her with "a problem". Leaving that for the moment, Webb continued, "Did your sister also resent her?"

"Yes. She thought she was far too bossy."

"Yet she was upset to hear of her death."

Henry was silent, but Webb persisted. "Were you surprised by her reaction?"

He moved uneasily. "I was a bit. It must have been the shock."

Yes, Jackson thought, shock—and fear. They, rather than grief, might account for her tears. But why should Rose be afraid?

"You work in your father's hotel?"

92

"Only in the vac. I'm studying Hotel and Catering Management at Guildford."

"And what does your sister do?"

"She's at Broadminster Art School. She wants to be a sculptor."

A sculptor needs strong hands, Webb thought, and Nancy'd only a little neck. He changed tack. "Did Mrs. Pendrick spend time with anyone particular at the party last weekend?"

"No, she was moving round being sociable."

"Did any of the guests come from Shillingham or that direction?"

"I don't think so. They were nearly all local, except my uncle and aunt and a friend of Dad's from Oxford."

"So you can't account for her being in Shillingham?"

"Not at all. When she'd made such a fuss about the short week, why come back again the next day?"

"You realize, then, that she died on Wednesday?"

Henry's eyes flew to his face. "You told Mrs. Foldes it's the Chedbury case."

So he at least had read the item. "Did you suspect it might be?"

"Of course I didn't. I told you, we were convinced she was in London."

"Where were you on Wednesday afternoon?" The question came casually and Henry didn't immediately see its significance. Then he flushed and answered too quickly.

"Helping the pastry chef."

Webb nodded at Jackson, who made a note to check with the hotel.

"Is there anything at all you can tell us, which might be useful?"

"No, nothing. Sorry."

It could be the truth. His approach to Nancy might be irrelevant but Webb would have preferred him to mention it. Perhaps, after reflection, he would. Webb let it ride for now.

"Then that's all for the time being, thank you. Sergeant, see if the young lady can spare us a moment."

"I'll get her," Henry offered, but Webb shook his head. "Don't worry, sir. Sergeant Jackson will ask the housekeeper."

Henry shrugged and followed Jackson out of the room. Webb sat back in his chair, looking round the room. Patio doors

94

led to a large, well-tended garden, drab at this season but with plants and bushes neatly trimmed for spring. No doubt the hotel gardener looked after it.

He remembered the years of his marriage, and Susan's insistence on his mowing the lawn, no matter how tired he was. "What will the neighbours think?" she'd ask. As if he cared.

There was the sound of footsteps and Rose Pendrick came through the arch, followed by Jackson. She'd recovered her composure. Her eyes were dry and gave no sign of recent tears.

"You wanted to see me? Chief Inspector, isn't it?"

"That's right, miss."

She sat on the sofa and regarded him steadily, not a frightened girl looking at a police officer, but a woman looking at a man. He cleared his throat.

"Now, Miss Pendrick, I know you're upset and I'll make this as brief as possible. Have you any idea why your stepmother was killed?"

A tremor shook her and she caught her lip between her teeth. But her eyes didn't leave his. "None at all."

I don't believe her, Webb thought. She knows something, but she's no intention of telling us.

"Was she popular in the village?"

"She was hardly ever here."

"But when she was, she and your father entertained."

"Sometimes, but they're Daddy's friends. His and—my mother's."

"When did your mother die, Miss Pendrick?"

"Four years ago."

And it was three since Pendrick remarried. He could understand her resentment. "Did she have a long illness?"

"No illness at all. She fell downstairs and broke her neck."

Pendrick was unlucky with his wives. "I'm very sorry. To return to your stepmother, can you think of anything that would bring her to Shillingham midweek?"

Again the flicker, followed by an emphatic shake of her head. "Nothing."

"When did you last speak to her?"

"I didn't see her after Monday evening."

"Finally, Miss Pendrick, can you tell me

what you were doing between four and six on Wednesday afternoon?"

Her knuckles clenched but she answered calmly. "Sculpting in my room. It was some holiday work I'd been set."

"Can anyone confirm that?"

"No one checked up on me, if that's what you mean."

"Do you drive, Miss Pendrick?"

"Naturally. I've my own car."

"But you didn't go to Shillingham that afternoon?"

"I did not."

"All right, miss. That's all, thank you."

Her eyes moved slowly and deliberately over him. Then, without a word, she rose and left the room.

Jackson gave a low whistle. "You'd better watch it, Guv! I think she fancies you!"

"I'm old enough to be her father."

"So? She's quite something, though, isn't she?"

"She is indeed, Ken."

More footsteps, and this time Mrs. Foldes appeared bearing a tray, which she set on the coffee table. "Mr. Pendrick thought you'd be more comfortable in here, sir. If there's anything you want, just let me know."

A nice distinction, Webb thought ironically. Not invited to eat with the family, whose low voices now reached him from the dining area, but not sent to the kitchen, either. Or perhaps, to do Pendrick justice, he had assumed they'd want to talk privately.

He sampled the pie. Despite Mrs. Foldes's distraction, it was very good. "When we've eaten, we'll take a look at Mrs. Pendrick's things and have a word with the housekeeper. Then we'll go to the hotel and try to discover where the ex-husband buzzed off to."

Jackson felt in his pocket. "When I went for the girl, Mr. Pendrick gave me this. It's a list of the party guests, with their addresses."

"Thanks." Webb laid it beside his plate and glanced at it casually. Then he stiffened. The third name down was Miss Charlotte Yates. "*A friend of Dad's from Oxford.*"

"My God!" he said softly.

"What is it, Guv?"

Webb tapped the list with his knife.

"There's a lady here whom I met last Sunday."

Jackson grinned. "Didn't know you moved in such circles! Reckon she did it?"

"No, but I'd certainly like to speak to her. I'd no idea she knew the Pendricks." Perhaps Hannah did, too. Webb's mind started racing.

"She might have noticed something," Jackson said hopefully.

"Too true. If there was anything to notice, she'd notice it all right."

The bedroom to which they were led after lunch contained predominantly Pendrick's things. "As you see, Chief Inspector, there's little of Nancy's here. The London flat was still her real home."

It took only minutes to flick through the few underclothes, a jumper or two and some catering magazines. There were no personal papers. It occurred to Jackson that if there had been, there'd been opportunity enough, during the interviews and lunch, for Oliver Pendrick to remove them.

"Not much here, as you say." Webb turned back to Pendrick, who was watching them from the doorway. "We'll need to examine the clothes you were wearing on Wednesday. It's for elimination really, but it gives us a starting point. So if you could collect them together and ask your son and daughter to do the same, I'd be very grateful. They'll be returned as soon as the lab's finished with them."

He didn't like that, Webb thought. They never did. However innocent they were, they feared some terrible secret might be revealed under analysis.

"We'll call back when we've been to the hotel, but first we'll have a quick word with Mrs. Foldes, if that's all right."

The housekeeper had little to contribute. She'd been with the Pendricks for twenty years and since neither wife had tried to usurp her kitchen, she'd been content. She respectfully made it clear that, police or no police, she'd no intention of discussing her employers with them. In any case, the Pendricks were unlikely to have conducted their arguments in her presence. It was a necessary but unfruitful interview, and when it was completed the two men walked across the road to the hotel.

Known internationally for its comfort

and cuisine, The Gables took a murder inquiry in its stride. Interviews were held discreetly in Pendrick's office, but the staff hadn't known Nancy and couldn't add to Webb's knowledge of her. There was, however, one positive outcome. Dean had indeed left a note of his whereabouts, and the receptionist handed it over.

Webb glanced at it and passed it without comment to Jackson. It was an address in Shillingham.

"Well, lad," he said ten minutes later, as he fastened his seat-belt, "I'll give you three guesses where we're going now."

"Eleven Jubilee Road."

"Got it in one!"

The humbler residents of Shillingham lived near the railway. Along Station Road were the cheaper chain stores and discount warehouses, while behind the station, small terraced houses and working men's clubs crowded together in enforced intimacy. The crisscross of narrow streets bore such names as Trafalgar, Waterloo and Balaclava. Which jubilee was commemorated, Jackson didn't know—he suspected Victoria's—but he knew where to find it, since one of his informers lived there. As he switched off the engine outside No. 11, the roar of the crowd reached them from the nearby football stadium.

"United are playing at home," he told Webb. "Bob will be in there rooting!"

Sergeant Dawson was a fanatical supporter of the home team.

"Never mind, you'll get a blow by blow account on Monday."

Iron railings had once graced the low wall, but in keeping with their proud name, the residents of Jubilee Road had, during the war, sent them to be melted for munitions. The scars still remained, unsightly bumps on the cracked, uneven brickwork.

The two men walked up the path. Webb raised the tarnished knocker and let it fall. The door was opened by a faded woman in bedroom slippers, who regarded them suspiciously.

"Good afternoon," Webb said pleasantly. "Is Mr. Dean at home?"

Her face closed. "No he isn't, more's the pity, since he owes a week's rent."

"You mean he's left?"

"Cleared off without a word."

"When was this, Mrs—?"

"Tallow's the name. Wednesday night, it was, and not a whisper beforehand, never mind a week's notice."

Webb's voice was expressionless. "Could we come in for a moment? I'm Chief Inspector Webb and this is Sergeant Jackson."

"I don't want no trouble with the police."

"We're only trying to trace Mr. Dean. Don't you want to yourself."

"Yes. Well." Grudgingly she stepped aside and they went into the dark passage. Pushing open the door, she showed them into an equally dark front room, any light that might have filtered through being kept at bay by dirty net curtains.

Noting the greasy chairs, Webb elected to remain standing. "Can you think of any reason why he went off like that?"

She sniffed. "Well, he had a ding-dong fight with his ladyfriend. I could hear them in the kitchen, shouting at each other."

"What lady was that, Mrs. Tallow?"

"Don't know her name, do I? I mean,

he didn't *introduce* us." Her voice was heavy with sarcasm. "It wasn't the usual one, anyway."

"Do you know if he was expecting her?"

"Yes, she rang the night before—he told me at supper. 'Make us a pot of tea, will you?' he said. So I did, and they never touched it, neither of them. Found it stewed in the pot, and not even milk in the cups."

"Was he worried by the phone call?"

"Didn't seem to be. Couldn't have known what was coming."

"What kind of lady was she?"

"Posh. Well-spoken. Too good for the likes of him. Lovely fur jacket she had."

Webb avoided Jackson's eye. "What time did she get here?"

"Bit after four. Only stayed about ten minutes."

"Did they leave together?"

"Bless you, no. She slammed out the door and he slammed upstairs. And that was the last I saw of him. I got the four-forty as usual—"

Webb leaned forward. "You went out?"

"Like I said. Every Wednesday, week

in and week out. I go to Vi's for tea, then on to Bingo."

"Where do you catch the bus, Mrs. Tallow?"

"Corner of Dick Lane. The number forty-seven."

"So you left the house soon after she did?"

"Couldn't have been more than five minutes. I left his supper for him like I always did, but when I got back it was still in the oven and he'd gone. Waste of good food, I call it."

"And he'd taken all his things with him?"

"Every last tittle."

"May we see his room?"

"What's the point? There's nothing in it."

And she was right. She stood in the doorway with folded arms as they turned drawers upside down and felt along the top of the wardrobe.

"Satisfied?" she asked with a sniff.

"Thank you for your help, Mrs. Tallow. An officer will be round shortly to lift any fingerprints. He'll try not to disturb you. And of course if Mr. Dean should contact you, or you remember anything that might be useful, please ring us at the station."

He wasn't hopeful. Mrs. Tallow and her kind didn't "hold" with the police.

"How about that, then?" Jackson said with satisfaction as they got into the car. "Stroke of luck, wasn't it? Bet he regrets leaving a forwarding address!"

"Unfortunately," Webb said drily, "he didn't leave one this time."

"Reckon it was him though, don't you, Guv?"

"Let's just say I wouldn't be in his shoes."

Dusk thickened the air as they turned into Station Road. "London tomorrow," Webb said. "We'll have to look over the flat. If she left in a hurry, it might tell us something. Phone Hampstead when we get back, and ask them to fix accommodation."

"We'll be staying overnight?"

"Afraid so. The catering place won't be open till Monday, and we'll have to see the Beresfords, which'll mean a trip to Surrey. When you've done that, Ken, ring Mr. Pendrick for a full description of Dean and get it into circulation. If he has a record, we can match up the prints. I'll check on Pendrick's car and arrange for Dean's room to get the once-over."

When Webb left his office an hour later he was still on duty, but at least business could now be mixed with pleasure. He had to see Hannah and learn what he could about Miss Yates and the Pendricks.

6

"**D**AVID! Come in. Are you free this evening?"

He kissed her, feeling some of his tiredness seep away. "I shall be, but first I have to ask you some questions."

She looked at him quickly and he wondered what she read in his face. She went ahead of him into the sitting-room, drawing the curtains on the outer darkness.

"All right," she said quietly, seating herself opposite him. "What's happened?"

He rubbed a hand across his face. "You've not had the news on today?"

"No?"

"The woman who was found at Chedbury has been identified. I'm sorry to tell you it was Nancy Pendrick."

Her eyes filled with horror, and for a moment he was reminded of Rose. "Nancy Pendrick? But that's terrible. She was a friend of my aunt's."

"I know. Had you ever met her?"

Hannah shook her head, eyes still wide with concern. "Charlotte was telling me about them last weekend. She—" She gripped the arms of her chair. "David, she's up there now. In Nancy's flat. She won't know anything about this."

He came to his feet. "You're sure?"

"It was arranged at the party, so she could go round the sales."

"Damn!"

"Does it matter?"

"I wanted to see the place as Mrs. Pendrick left it." He thought rapidly. "When was your aunt going up, do you know?"

"On Friday. Nancy gave her the key, in case they missed each other."

"Have you got the phone number?"

As she shook her head, the phone started to ring. Hannah went to answer it and he relaxed slightly at her opening words.

"I've just this moment heard—I can't believe it. David's here. I think he'd like a word with you."

She turned, her hand over the mouthpiece. "It was on the early evening news."

He took the phone from her. "Miss

109

Yates? Webb here. I'm sorry about this. How long were you intending to stay?"

Charlotte's voice reached him, less firm than usual. "Till tomorrow afternoon. I'd hoped to see some exhibitions, but now—"

"I'll be up in the morning, and it'd be a great help if you could stay till I get there."

A pause. Then, as she steadied herself, "Very well, Chief Inspector, I'll wait for you."

"Thank you. I'll be with you soon after ten. In the meantime, I'll hand you back to Hannah."

He returned to the fire, assessing the new development. After a few minutes, Hannah joined him.

"I've asked her to come here. She shouldn't be alone—she's had a bad shock." She looked up at him gravely. "You won't bully her, will you, David?"

"It'd take a better man than me to bully Miss Yates! How long has she known Nancy?"

"Five years. It was she who introduced her to Oliver."

"Before or after his first wife was killed?"

Remembering Charlotte's conjectures, Hannah caught her breath. They were unpleasantly relevant now. "Soon after," she answered in a low voice.

Her brief pause made Webb uneasy. "You'd been talking about the Pendricks. Can you remember what was said?"

"It was just a recap, really, on how long she'd known them. Nothing important."

"It's important to me, Hannah. That New Year party is all we have to go on, and Miss Yates was there. She could have noticed something without realizing its significance."

"Then I'm afraid you must ask her yourself. Her remarks were off-the-cuff and she might be wishing now she hadn't made them."

"But it's the first reaction I want, not a censored version! Why do people always clam up in a murder case? Misguided loyalty, I suppose." As she remained silent, he added more gently, "Did something strike her as wrong?"

"She thought Nancy and Oliver'd had a row," Hannah said unwillingly.

That, he knew. Nevertheless, he said, "Why was that?"

"Oh, I don't know, David. You'll have to ask Charlotte. It was only an impression."

"You're not very helpful, are you? What do you think I'll do, rush off half-cocked and arrest someone on your say-so? I'm trying to get the feel of the case, that's all, get to know the dead woman. *Somebody* killed her, dammit. Don't you want us to discover who?"

He turned away, running a hand over his hair. "I'm sorry. You're upset and I shouldn't shout at you. But I think you know more than you're saying, and after a long day I resent it."

After a moment, Hannah said, "Have you been out at Frecklemarsh?"

"Yes."

"It's a pretty little place, isn't it?"

"Not my cup of tea." He smiled wryly. "I'm not trying to be difficult, I just don't like it. Give me the solid earthiness of Otterford or Larksworth. Frecklemarsh is a pseudo-village, where rich businessmen pretend to be farmers."

"A *Petit Trianon*?" Hannah suggested.

"What?"

"Where Marie Antoinette played at milkmaids."

"You teachers! Yes, that kind of thing. And since The Gables is a popular place to take foreigners, no doubt there are hundreds of Germans and Frenchmen and Americans who think it's a typical English village."

"I'm fond of it, but then I'm prejudiced. It was my grandparents' home and I loved going to stay with them."

"So your mother and aunt were brought up there?"

"Yes, but it wasn't so built up then. Charlotte hardly knew anyone at the party, except the Beresfords."

"How does she know them?"

"Their parents were friends. They played together as children."

Again he sensed omission and again it irritated him. He'd never before found Hannah less than open, but it seemed she was honouring her aunt's confidence. Still, he'd find out tomorrow. Bullying or not, he'd brook no prevarication from Charlotte Yates.

Meanwhile, since the atmosphere was

not conducive to a relaxed evening, he would cut his losses and retire upstairs.

He said, "I'm sorry to have been the bearer of bad news, but I'll leave you in peace now."

She didn't try to detain him, merely nodded and saw him to the door. He paused for a moment, looking down into her grave, troubled eyes. "Good night, Hannah."

"Good night."

She waited till he reached the foot of the stairs, then closed the door behind him.

At Gables Lodge, Rose lay on her bed staring at the ceiling. Her face was streaked with tears, her breathing laboured from recent sobbing. You bastard! she thought. You rotten, murdering bastard! Then, with a renewed upsurge of tears, Oh Nancy, I'm sorry, I'm sorry! I never meant this to happen!

Charlotte Yates opened the door. She was dressed in a black wool dress with a high neck, black stockings and suede boots. As before, her only ornament was the jade pendant.

"Come in, Chief Inspector. And Sergeant, is it? There's some coffee ready. You must have made an early start."

"Thank you." They followed her down the minute hall to the living-room. It was pleasantly cluttered, a comfortable, lived-in room vibrant with the personality of its owner. On the desk stood a photograph in a silver frame. Webb walked over to look at it. It was of Nancy and Oliver on their wedding day.

He said without turning, "You were at the wedding, of course?"

"I was, but why of course?" She held out a coffee cup and he took it from her, seating himself in an easy chair. From the corner of his eye he saw Jackson ready with his pocket book.

"Hannah told me you'd introduced the bride and groom."

"I see."

And that, he reflected, was about all Hannah had told him, though he wouldn't let Miss Yates know that. If she thought her comments had already been passed on, she might be more forthcoming.

"You'd known them both some time?"

"Oliver and I both grew up in

Frecklemarsh, but I didn't know him well till he married my friend, Avis Beresford."

"And was that marriage happy, do you think?" Webb's voice was casual, but he was watching her carefully and caught her swift glance. No doubt she was wondering how much Hannah had told him.

"They were deeply in love, but that doesn't necessarily make for a happy marriage."

"There was jealousy?"

"I'm not a psychologist, Chief Inspector. I just know that at times both were intensely miserable. Such times may occur in all marriages; I'm not in a position to know."

"And this last one?"

"Hannah may have told you," Charlotte said with dry emphasis, "that I was surprised by their decision to marry, particularly on Nancy's part. But Oliver's an attractive man and I imagine she was flattered by his attentions. He's also successful, which is a quality Nancy admired. After her singularly unsuccessful first husband, that may well have swayed the balance."

116

"What kind of woman was she? We need to build up a picture of her."

Charlotte stirred her coffee thoughtfully. "If one characteristic outshone the others, it was her honesty. She was completely straightforward herself and wouldn't countenance underhandedness in others. She was also outspoken, which caused the odd ripple from time to time. For instance, she'd tell a chef to his face that his sauce was a disaster. You were never in doubt as to her opinion of you."

"Please go on, Miss Yates. This is just what we need."

"She was self-reliant: she'd had to be, both as a young girl and during her first marriage. Because of that, she gave the impression of bossiness, of wanting to 'manage' people. She could be generous, but she'd a ruthless streak, particularly if her principles were involved. If someone had done wrong, it would be no use asking her to keep quiet."

She smiled reflectively. "On one occasion she even turned Danny over to the police."

"For what?"

"Burglary, I think. She wanted to teach

him a lesson. He went to prison for six months, but apparently bore no grudges. When he came out, she took him back and the matter wasn't mentioned again."

"Which says something for both of them. Did she make enemies?"

Charlotte shook her head. "That's too strong a word. As I say, she didn't waste time on tact, but there was no malice in her."

Despite her disclaimer, Webb doubted if a psychologist could have given a fuller analysis.

"Thank you, Miss Yates, that was very helpful. Now, I'd like you to think carefully. When you arrived here on Friday, was there anything to suggest Mrs. Pendrick intended returning to the flat before your visit?"

"Do you know, there was, now I think of it. For one thing, her lunch dishes were in the sink, which surprised me."

"There was only one plate?"

"Yes."

"Could you tell what she'd eaten?"

"Beans on toast, I think. There were crumbs by the toaster, and an empty tin in the waste-bin." Which confirmed

Stapleton's findings. "And although the guest-room bed was made up, there were no clean towels. Also, her toilet things were in the bathroom—toothbrush and so on. I assumed she'd two sets and kept one at Frecklemarsh."

"No scribbled message by the phone?"

"I didn't look."

"Then let's look now."

His hunch was correct. On the pad by the telephone, a Shillingham number had been jotted down. He'd check, but he was sure it was Mrs. Tallow's. Also on the table lay an engagement diary. Webb and Jackson, leaning over it together, exchanged a glance. An appointment for Wednesday afternoon had been scored through. At Webb's nod, Jackson tore the top sheet from the pad and put it and the diary in his pocket. They returned to their seats and the questioning resumed.

"Now, Miss Yates, the party last weekend. I gather you felt the atmosphere was strained?"

"Hannah again?"

Treacherously he did not defend her, though he sensed Charlotte's annoyance. She said levelly, "These people are my

119

friends, Chief Inspector. I don't care to discuss them with strangers."

"So was Mrs. Pendrick your friend, and she was murdered. One of the others might have done it."

He saw that he'd shaken her.

"I thought it was a mugger, someone like that."

"I doubt it. Something important took her to Broadshire. She'd complained about the short week, yet she was back in Shillingham on Wednesday afternoon, and met her death there. Why, and at whose hand?"

Charlotte's long, ringless fingers toyed with her pendant, but she made no comment.

"So," Webb continued deliberately, "anything, no matter how vague, that you can tell me about that party could be of great value."

Her eyes, large and grey and uncannily like Hannah's, held his. "You really think her murderer could have been there?"

"I'd say it's very probable. So please, what made you feel something was wrong?" The reason Pendrick had given was not necessarily the true one.

She gave a shrug. "You know how it is when people have had a row. They were over-polite to each other and gushing to everyone else. And they kept away from each other. Later, when the Fraynes arrived, I thought that might have been the reason for it."

"The Fraynes?"

"The new doctor and his wife. Mrs. Frayne was once engaged to Oliver."

"Is that so? What happened, do you know?"

"Twenty-five years ago? It's a familiar story. Avis set her cap at him, he fell wildly in love with her, ditched his fiancée and married her, all within the space of six weeks."

"He goes in for hasty marriages, doesn't he? And they were all quite friendly at the party?"

"As far as I could see."

So Pendrick, who admitted to a row with his wife, had come face to face with a woman he'd once loved. And four days later, Nancy was murdered.

"Did you notice anything else at the party? Anyone who seemed on edge, uncomfortable in any way?"

"I don't think so. Dr. Frayne had too much to drink and had to be taken home. Otherwise there was nothing unusual."

"Who took him?"

"I don't remember their names. Two of Oliver's golfing friends. They came back after delivering him."

"Did Mrs. Pendrick talk with anyone in particular?"

"Not that I noticed."

"And you didn't hear her arrange to meet anyone during the week?"

"Definitely not." She added suddenly, "Oliver phoned yesterday, to see if Nancy was here."

"Did he sound worried?"

"No, just annoyed. He was surprised when I answered. Either she hadn't told him I was coming, or he'd forgotten."

"How well did you know Mrs. Pendrick's first husband?"

"Not at all. I didn't meet Nancy till they'd separated."

"Did you know he was recently working at The Gables?"

"Danny Dean was? How odd."

"Mrs. Pendrick didn't mention it, then?"

"Not to me, but I hadn't seen her for some time. I'm surprised Oliver allowed it."

"At first he didn't realize who he was. Then his wife persuaded him to give Dean a chance."

"Yes," Charlotte said reflectively, "that sounds like Nancy."

"One final question, Miss Yates, for the record. Where were you last Wednesday afternoon?"

She returned his gaze. "In Oxford, Chief Inspector. Playing bridge, actually. I hardly ever play, but I did, thank God, last Wednesday. I can supply names for corroboration."

"If you would."

She went to the telephone table and wrote on the pad. Then she handed the list to Webb.

"For the record," she said.

"Thank you. Now, we'll take a look round before leaving, in case there's anything we've missed."

But the flat had nothing more to tell them. They returned to the living-room, where Charlotte was waiting.

"Thank you, Miss Yates, you've been

very helpful, and I'm grateful to you for staying till we got here. One last favour: do you by any chance know the Beresfords' phone number?"

"Yes, of course. It's in my diary." She lifted the heavy handbag he'd seen before.

"I believe they're old friends of yours?"

"Roger is, certainly. He was Avis's twin."

"I didn't know that. He must have felt her death very deeply."

"We all did." She found the number and read it out to him.

"I'll phone them now, if you'll excuse me, and make an appointment."

The voice from Chardsey informed him that Mr. and the Honourable Mrs. Beresford were spending the weekend in London. They needn't go to Surrey after all. Webb dialled again. A woman's voice answered, high-pitched and upper-class.

"Mrs. Beresford?" (Honourable, my fanny!)

"Speaking, yes."

He identified himself. "I'm in London at the moment and I'd be grateful for a word with you both. What time would be convenient?"

There was a slight pause. "I'm afraid we're just going out to lunch."

"When will you be back, madam?"

"About three-thirty, I should think." Another pause. "It's to do with poor dear Nancy, I suppose?"

"That's right, madam. We'll be along at three-thirty, then."

He turned from the phone to see Charlotte in her coat, holding her suitcase. "Hannah insists I go to her, bless her. I've certainly had enough of my own company in the last twelve hours."

Jackson took the case from her and they left the flat together. After she'd locked the door, Charlotte handed Webb the key. "You'd better take charge of this." He nodded his thanks.

Her car was in a garage in the side street facing the flat. "Goodbye, Chief Inspector. No doubt we'll meet again."

She nodded to Jackson, and they stood watching as she manoeuvred the car past those lining the road, their own among them.

"What did you make of her, Ken?"

"Tough, self-confident, a bit haughty. Wouldn't like to get on her wrong side."

"True. I like her, though. Well, we'll have to kick our heels till three-thirty. God, how I hate London, specially on Sundays. Let's call on the local Force. We ought to put them in the picture, specially since they've fixed our accommodation for us. Then we can have a bite of lunch."

7

THEY located the Beresfords through the *A to Z*. In one of London's most opulent squares, their flat was the ground floor of a large Georgian house.

Roger Beresford opened the door himself. His face, Webb thought, was a middle-aged schoolboy's, lined but still young-looking, with an expression of anxious friendliness. Webb could almost see him in cap and blazer.

"So sorry to keep you waiting," he said as he led them to the drawing-room. "Some friends from South Africa were giving a lunch party."

"No problem, sir."

Faith Beresford was standing at the fireplace—a deliberate pose, Webb was willing to bet. Her short hair and boyish figure were set off by her Twenties-style dress, with its flat bodice and dropped waist. Unlike Miss Yates, she wore a set of gold bangles and a large sapphire ring.

Introductions were performed and Webb sat gingerly on a brocade chair. Jackson chose an upright, balancing his notebook on his knee.

"Did you come all this way to see us, Chief Inspector?" Beresford inquired easily. "You were lucky to catch us in town."

"We've been to Mrs. Pendrick's flat, sir. Miss Yates was spending the weekend there."

"God, yes. I heard them arranging it at New Year. Poor Charlotte—was she very upset?"

"She was shaken, naturally. She's known Mrs. Pendrick for some time."

"That's right, longer than any of us. But it's shaken us all. A terrible thing to have happened."

"I believe you were in Broadshire yourselves, sir, last weekend. Did Mr. and Mrs. Pendrick seem happy together?"

Faith gave what in anyone less ladylike would have been a snort. "They fought like cat and dog the whole weekend."

"Oh darling, steady! That's not quite true!"

"Of course it's true, Roger. It took them

128

all their time to be civil at the party, and there was that unpleasant scene the next day."

"What scene was that, Mrs. Beresford?"

"Oliver complained Nancy was never there, and she accused him of neglecting his family. Then for some reason Henry took umbrage and started shouting too. I don't remember the details, but it was all very vulgar and gave me quite a headache."

That tallied with Oliver's account.

"I understand Mr. Pendrick's ex-fiancée was at the party. Did his wife know who she was?"

"I've no idea." It was Roger who answered. "I imagine she must have."

"But their edginess wasn't because of her?"

"I don't think so. As my wife said, it stemmed from the time Nancy spent in London." He hesitated. "I shouldn't pay too much attention to it, Chief Inspector. It would probably all have blown over if poor Nancy hadn't been killed."

"You could be right, sir," Webb said blandly. "Now, I understand you were in Shillingham on Wednesday afternoon?"

"Wednesday? Yes, we were. Faith had a hair appointment."

"What time would that have been?"

Beresford glanced at his wife. "Three o'clock, wasn't it? It was a long do, because she had some beauty treatment as well—massage or something."

Mrs. Beresford, disliking this discussion of her affairs, nodded confirmation.

"Could you tell me which—er—salon it was, madam?"

She raised her eyebrows. "Alexander's, in East Parade. I always go there when I'm over."

"And you were there from three o'clock till when?"

"It must have been five-fifteen or so, wasn't it, Roger?"

"Too darned long, certainly. I got frozen, hanging about."

"And what did you do, sir, while your wife was engaged?"

Roger stared at him for a moment. Then he said softly, "My God, are we talking about the time Nancy died?"

"That's right, sir."

"But wasn't it Thursday she was found? I hadn't—"

"She'd been dead over twenty-four hours. The time of death was between four and six p.m. on the fourth."

"My God!" Beresford said again. His eyes came back to Webb's. "I'm sorry, you asked what I was doing. I went to the cinema, Chief Inspector. The Odeon, in Gloucester Circus."

"What programme was showing, sir?"

"The Magnificent Seven—for the Christmas holidays, I suppose. I can tell you the plot in detail, but since I've seen it three times, it's not much of an alibi."

"You saw the complete programme?"

"No, it had been on about an hour when I got there. I was only filling in time till Faith was ready. As it was, she was later than I expected."

"You collected her from the salon?"

"Yes, she didn't know where the car was."

"And where was it?"

"In the Odeon car park."

"So you didn't use the Duke Street multi-storey?"

"No, why?"

"Mrs. Pendrick parked there that afternoon."

Roger's face was white. "I could have bumped into her! God, if only I had!"

"Did you see anyone you knew in Shillingham?"

"Only Henry, in the distance."

"Henry Pendrick?"

"Yes. He was across the road as I came out of the cinema. I don't think he saw me."

"And that would have been when?"

"Just after five, I'd say."

Interesting. According to Henry—and his father—he'd been in the hotel kitchens. "Have you got the car with you now, sir?"

"No, we came up by train. I never drive in London if I can help it."

"I take it you'd have no objection if we ask the local Force to examine it?"

Roger gave a nervous laugh. "None at all, but I doubt if it'll be much use. It was filthy after all that country mud, and I left instructions for it to be given a good clean and polish."

"Nevertheless, sir, it's routine procedure, as I'm sure you appreciate. And I'm afraid I'll also have to take the clothes you were wearing on Wednesday. That, too, is standard practice."

Faith Beresford said on a high note, "You don't want *my* clothes, I hope?"

"I'm sorry, madam. It's a formality, but we can't make exceptions."

"Then you'd better take care of them," she said tightly, "or I'll claim for damages."

Beresford threw Webb an apologetic glance. "I'm afraid that'll fall to the local Force, too; we only have formal clothes here. I'll phone through and leave instructions."

"Thank you, sir. I'm sorry to have disturbed your Sunday."

"Well, Ken," Webb said drily as they drove out of the square, "you've met your first 'Hon'. What did you think of her?"

"Seemed a cold fish, didn't she? Shouldn't think he has much of a life with her."

"Depends what he's prepared to settle for. She's decorative and rich and has influence in the right places. Earl's daughter, and all that."

Jackson dismissed Faith's assets with a grunt. "I liked him, though. Seemed a decent sort of bloke. Bit of a novelty for him, wasn't it, being on the wrong end of the questioning?"

The next morning, the staff at Dean Catering seemed generally more upset than the Pendricks. Perhaps they'd been closer to Nancy than her own family. But for all their grief, they'd little to tell. She had returned as expected on Tuesday, seeming her usual efficient self. She'd also come in on Wednesday, but cancelled an appointment for the afternoon.

"I was surprised," said the manageress. "It wasn't like her—she hated breaking appointments."

"She gave no reason?"

"Said something important had come up, so would I change it to Thursday."

"She expected to be back the next day, then?"

"Oh yes. She asked for some papers to be on her desk first thing."

"So what did you think when she didn't turn up?"

"I couldn't understand it. I kept ringing the flat, but there was no reply. So I thought she must have been delayed and would get back as soon as she could."

"She didn't say where she was going?"

"No. I didn't realize it was out of London."

"What time did she leave here on Wednesday?"

"Just after midday. Said she wanted an early lunch."

Webb tapped his pencil reflectively. "Had she any men-friends, do you know?"

"She never mentioned any, but then she wouldn't, would she?"

"You don't know how she spent her free time?"

"When the school was open, she did a lot of preparation for that."

"Did you ever meet her first husband?"

"Mr. Dean? He's been in once or twice. Looking for a hand-out, I shouldn't wonder. I don't know why she bothers with him."

"You think she gave him money?"

"I'm blooming sure she did. She was soft like that." The woman's eyes filled with tears, and she dabbed at them with a handkerchief.

"Could you describe him for us?"

"Oh, he's nice enough looking. Fancies himself no end. Dark, wavy hair—going thin on top, but he brushes it over the bald patch. Quite a one for the ladies."

"Age?"

She shrugged. "Mid-forties, I suppose."

"And how tall is he?"

"Medium—not as tall as you."

"Eyes?"

She thought for a moment. "Blue, I think. Yes, blue."

Webb came to his feet. "Thank you, Mrs. Carstairs. We'll be in touch if there's anything else."

Frost still lay in the shadows as they came down the steps, but the strengthening sun glinted on the pavements.

"Well, Ken," Webb said with relief, "we've done all we came for. Let's head for home. We can fill ourselves in on the latest before the inquest. Did that description tally with Pendrick's?"

"More or less. You reckon Dean's the one we're after?"

"We're after him all right, but whether he's guilty is anyone's guess. Lord love us, a husband and ex-husband in one case!

136

Too much of a good thing, wouldn't you say?"

They were back in Shillingham by one o'clock, and, having left the car in Carrington Street, walked round the corner to The Brown Bear. Inspector Crombie raised his fork in greeting.

"The wanderers return! How's the Big City?"

"Big." Webb sat down while Jackson went for drinks.

"Worth the trip?"

"Oh, I think so. Nothing spectacular, but the facts are building up. I reckon we can narrow the time of death to between four-thirty and five."

"How d'you arrive at that?"

"Well, according to the stomach contents, she'd eaten four hours before death. We now know that last meal was in London. She'd left her office around twelve saying she wanted an early lunch, and the remains of it were still in the flat when Miss Yates arrived. I'd say she ate between twelve-thirty and one and left soon afterwards—she didn't stop to wash up.

"Allowing for traffic getting through

London and so on, the journey should take roughly two hours and forty minutes. At any rate we know she was at the car park at four, and Jubilee Road soon after. And according to Mrs. Tallow she left at four-twenty. So, taking the time of death as four hours after eating, we come up with four-thirty to five. QED."

"Wonderful!" said Crombie, in mock admiration.

Jackson put three pints of beer on the table. "Pie and chips, Guv?"

"Fine. Thanks, Ken." Jackson went back to the bar and Webb drank from his tankard. "It may be circumstantial but it fits the facts. You know, Alan, there's one thing worrying me. She was in Broadshire the previous week; why didn't she see Dean then? Why go all the way to London and have to come dashing back?"

"Perhaps she didn't want to see him earlier."

"Then what changed her mind? Why was it suddenly so urgent it couldn't wait till Friday, when she'd be back anyway? Remember, he didn't contact her, it was she who phoned him. Mrs. Tallow was clear on that. And another thing. She came at some inconvenience specifically to see Dean. Having seen him, wouldn't she have gone straight back to the car and home again?"

"Perhaps she was making for it when she got waylaid."

"At four-thirty in the afternoon? With the streets still crowded with people?"

"Stranger things have happened."

"Any in the last twenty-four hours?"

"No, everything's been fairly routine. Dick returned Mr. Pendrick's car and is going over his kids'. I haven't heard his findings. And of course the Scirocco was done with a tooth comb, to no avail."

Jackson arrived with two steaming platesful and seated himself at the table. Webb reached for the salt.

"Ken, while I'm at the inquest, get on to CRO. We now know Dean has form: I want to see if there's a record of violence. Also, let Dick have that engagement book. We might as well confirm it was Nancy herself who scored out that appointment. And when he's checked it for dabs, make a note of all names and addresses, going back at least three months. Oh, and ask Mike Romilly at the *News* for a decko at reports on the first Mrs. Pendrick's death —inquest, PM, etcetera."

"What shall I do *after* tea, Guv?"

Webb grinned and piled some chips on his fork. "I'll think of something," he said.

It was five o'clock by the time Webb returned to the station and the Duty Sergeant called to him.

"Lady waiting for you, Guv. Been here over an hour, but wouldn't see anyone else. Got a little girl with her."

Webb glanced into the reception area. A middle-aged woman was perched on the edge of a chair, gripping her handbag with both hands. Beside her was a girl of about thirteen, with a long flaxen plait over one shoulder. He walked towards them.

"Good afternoon, madam. Webb, CID. You want to see me?"

"Oh yes, Inspector." She jumped to her feet and Webb made no comment on his demotion. "My little girl has something to tell you."

"We'll go to an interview room, then." He shepherded them across the wide hall to a vacant room, seated himself at the table, and gestured them to sit opposite. "Now, what can I do for you?"

"It's what *we* can do for *you*, Inspector," the woman said importantly.

"First, can I have your name and address?"

"Mrs. Robinson, 124, Wellington Street. And this is Sharon."

Webb smiled at the child, who seemed on the verge of tears. "Hello, Sharon."

"You see, Inspector, Sharon saw her. The lady that was murdered. On Wednesday afternoon." Having delivered her bombshell, she sat back with a pleased expression.

"Then you did right to come. Can you—"

"As soon as we saw her picture on telly, she gave a little scream, Sharon did. 'That's the lady!' she said, 'the one that was so kind.' So I said, 'Right. Down to the police we go.' We didn't even stop for tea, though the kettle had boiled."

"I hope the sergeant gave you some," Webb said diplomatically.

"Oh yes, he was very nice about it."

"Now, if Sharon could tell me in her own words—"

"She'd fallen down, see. I'm always telling her not to run, specially in the dark, but she won't be told. So she ran, and of course she fell, and this poor lady helped her up. Her last act of kindness, you might say."

Webb repressed a sigh. "Sharon, could you tell me exactly what happened?"

The child hung her head and sniffed.

"It was definitely Mrs. Pendrick you saw?" he prompted.

A nod.

"What time was this?"

"Dunno. About half four."

"And where were you?"

"In Station Road. I'd been to the Co-op for Mum."

It tied in. "And what happened?"

There was a long silence, then Mrs. Robinson said, "She's shy, but I told you, didn't I? She fell and this lady picked her up."

"Is that right, Sharon?"

Another nod.

"Did the lady speak to you?"

He had to bend his head to catch her reply. "She said, 'Whatever's the matter? Are you all right?'"

"Anything else?"

"I think she said, 'What happened?'"

"Think carefully, Sharon, this could be important. Was there anyone with the lady at the time—anyone at all?"

"No."

"You're quite sure of that?"

"Yes."

"Is it any help?" Mrs. Robinson asked eagerly.

In all conscience Webb couldn't see it was. It prolonged the last known appearance by some ten minutes, but that was all. However, he answered firmly, "Yes, I'm sure it is. I'm very grateful to you for coming. I'll arrange for a driver to run you home, and if Sharon remembers anything else, we'd be glad to hear about it."

"There!" said Mrs. Robinson with satisfaction. "I told you they'd want to know." And to Webb, "She didn't want to come, you know. Awful time I had with her, but I told her it was her duty."

The child's eyes were full of tears. It would be a shock, Webb thought, discovering someone she'd actually spoken to had been killed shortly after. And not by accident.

He stood looking after them as Mrs. Robinson bustled off with the driver, Sharon in tow.

"Any joy, Guv?" asked the Duty Sergeant.

"Not really, Andy. Another couple of minutes filled in, that's all." And he turned towards the stairs.

8

THE post mortem report, neatly typed, confirmed what Webb already knew. Nothing much under the fingernails. Gloves, he thought, should be banned. A policeman's life would be easier without them.

More interesting, though not relevant as far as he could see, was Dick Hodges's write-up on the cars. In Pendrick's, the passenger seat had offered up one dark hair, identified as belonging to a woman in her forties. Offhand, he could think of no one with hair that colour. Probably a friend or business contact. More surprising was the fact that, while one of his wife's hairs would not have been out of place, none had been found. Perhaps they shared each other's cars as little as everything else.

The reply was also through on Dean: he had served a six-month sentence for burglary in Brixton, being released in

November six years ago. There was no record of violence.

He pushed the reports away and stretched his long legs under the desk. Alan Crombie was filling in his diary, a worried crease between his brows as he struggled after an elusive memory.

"How are the new lads shaping?" Webb asked suddenly. "Haven't had a chance to see them yet."

Crombie removed his glasses and rubbed the bridge of his nose. "Eager as bloodhounds. Let's hope it lasts. Marshbanks has the edge on self-confidence—thanks to public school, I suppose."

"Spoken like a grammar-school boy!"

"Funny thing, he was at school with the Pendrick boy."

"Is that so? Wheel him in, will you, Alan? That might be useful."

Detective-Constable Marshbanks was twenty-two years old. He had an engagingly cheeky face, round brown eyes like boot buttons, and dark hair with a mind of its own. One quiff stood upright on the crown of his head, traces of dampness showing it had once been plastered down.

He stood stiffly to attention, his eyes fixed on the wall above Webb's head. Webb glanced at Crombie, saw the Inspector hide a smile.

"You can relax, lad. This is an informal chat."

"Yes, sir." The boy didn't move.

Webb kicked out a chair. "Take a pew."

"Thank you, sir."

"Inspector Crombie tells me you were at school with young Pendrick."

"Yes, sir."

"Where was that?"

"St. Benedict's, sir. In Broadminster."

"I know where St. Benedict's is." He didn't add it had featured in a murder case. "Did you know him well?"

"He was in my year, but not many of my classes. Athletic type. In all the teams, and pretty bright, too."

"Was he popular?"

A smile touched the boy's mouth. "Not particularly. We called him Henny-Penny."

"From his name, or a tendency to cluck?"

The smile broadened. "A bit of both."

"Did you like him?"

"He was all right, sir. Hadn't any sense of humour, though."

"Didn't like being Henny-Penny, for instance? Can't say I blame him. Any hobbies?"

"Well, sir, his main interest was horse-racing. He belonged to a betting circle."

Webb raised his eyebrows. "They ran a book at St. Benedict's?"

"After a fashion—very hush-hush, of course. Whenever they could, they skipped games and nipped off to the races."

"Had he any special friends?"

"There was a boy called Lingford. He ran the betting and egged the others on. At least, that's how it seemed to me."

"And where did he hail from?"

"He was a day boy, so he must have been fairly local."

"And you reckon Pendrick's hooked on gambling?"

"He was then, but that was four years ago."

"Once a gambler, always a gambler. I wonder if there are money problems. Worth following up. All right, Mr.

Marshbanks, that's all for the moment. No problems?"

"No, sir, thank you, sir."

"Nice lad," Webb commented as the young man left the room. "Take him under your wing, Alan. He could repay a bit of nurturing. Incidentally, Henry Pendrick was in Shillingham on Wednesday. Beresford saw him. About the crucial time, too."

"Wasn't he supposed to be at the hotel?"

"Quite. He'll have some explaining to do. And come to think of it, the sooner he gets on with it, the better." He lifted his phone. "Sergeant Jackson, please . . . Ken? On your bike, lad. We're Frecklemarsh bound."

"What worries me most," Mary Cudlip said, "is not giving her a decent burial."

Heather pushed back her hair. "It's *all* horrible. The village is crawling with reporters. Every time I go out, one of them stops me and asks if I knew Nancy."

"Poor love, what a start to your life here."

"I know it's selfish," Heather went on

in a low voice, "but it wouldn't seem so bad if I hadn't met her. And I shouldn't have done, but for the party. I wish we'd never gone. *God*, how I wish that!"

Mary looked at her with troubled sympathy. "If you're upset about Peter, don't be. He was overtired and he misjudged things. It's easily done, and no one will hold it against him."

But it was Oliver, not Peter, she'd been thinking of, as she had almost continuously since New Year. At least then the position was clear: he had a wife, and she a husband. Those minutes in the kitchen were a fluke, a non-happening. Press memory button and delete. But she couldn't, and nor, apparently, could he.

Last week, driven out of the house by restlessness, it had been no surprise to find him waiting. He'd opened the car door.

"We have to talk."

"Why?" She had stood, miserably defiant, her hair blowing across her face. "What is there to talk about?"

"You know as well as I do."

Oh yes, she knew. Knew the strength of her craving for him, the insistent clamour of her body that gave her no peace. But there was no point in discussing it.

They had, though, wearily and endlessly, driving round the dark lanes; and reached no conclusion. The obstacles were immovable. Or so it had seemed. Then came the news of Nancy's murder, and, most terrible of all, her first instinctive thought on hearing it: now Oliver's free!

Mary's voice brought her back. "You look pale, dear. Is there anything else worrying you?"

Heather shook her head, trying to smile. "Except that Joey's off to college next week. I'm really dreading it."

"You must be proud, though. I think it's wonderful, these girls training as doctors."

"But it's such a long course," Heather said shakily. "I'll miss her terribly."

"Yes, I remember when the boys left home. But before you know it, Easter will be here and she'll be back for the holidays."

"I know. I'm sorry to be so down, Mary. I don't know what's wrong with me."

151

"It's Peter's half-day, isn't it? Get him to take you to the cinema. That'll cheer you up."

But Peter, Heather knew, would spend the afternoon asleep in his chair. He always did. What would she do, she thought a little wildly, when Joey had gone and she'd no one to talk to? She switched on a bright smile. "Yes, that's a good idea."

"Don't let things get you down, dear. I know it's difficult at first, settling into a new place, and you've the added upheaval with Joanna. But things will fall into place, and in a couple of months you'll wonder what you were worried about." Mary picked up her bag. "I must be going, it's almost lunch-time. Don't forget supper on Thursday—we're looking forward to it."

As she prepared lunch, Heather fought an increasing sense of panic. She should never have come to Frecklemarsh, knowing Oliver was here. She'd tried to dissuade Peter, but his mother'd been ill and the frequent journeys between Ripon and Otterford were a strain on them all.

"Good God, girl!" he'd exclaimed, when she was forced to explain her reluctance.

"You can't go through life avoiding old flames! Anyway, it was years ago—he mightn't even recognize you."

He'd used the same argument when the invitation came. "Just take it in your stride, or he'll think you're still carrying a torch for him!" And he'd laughed at that.

And it *would* have been all right, she thought fiercely, if Oliver hadn't come upon her alone, if it hadn't been New Year's Eve, when kissing was a matter of course.

The front door banged and Peter came into the room. "I've just driven past the hotel—your boyfriend's still besieged by the Press. Not surprising, though, it's one of the penalties of getting rid of your wife!"

"Peter! For God's sake!"

He looked at her in surprise. "No need to get het up, I was only joking. Thank God I've a free afternoon." He flopped into a chair, loosening his tie. "Bring me a whisky, will you? I could do with a reviver."

"I'm just about to serve lunch."

"It can wait till I've had a drink. I'm in

need of one. The surgery was full of hysterical mothers."

She went to the dining-room and took the bottle from the sideboard. It was almost empty and she'd only bought it three days ago. She thought: I've got to get away! I'll have to convince Peter somehow. There must be other practices in the area.

"Hurry up with that drink—my throat's parched!"

She sloshed liquid into the glass and carried it back to the kitchen.

It was twelve-thirty as they rounded the bend on the approach to Frecklemarsh.

"Do you know," Webb said idly, "I once counted three private tennis courts from here."

"Rather have bowling myself." Jackson avoided a free-wheeling cyclist. "We won't be popular, arriving at lunch-time again."

"You're right. How'd you like an up-market pub lunch? The Dog and Gun's half way down on the left—pull in there. You'll probably get Brie with your Ploughman's, but it'll broaden your horizons!"

The prices at The Dog and Gun

reflected its social standing. Bloody hell! Jackson thought, as he studied the menu. They were mainly foreign dishes he couldn't pronounce, but he settled with relief for a baked potato. He was fond of that and they hadn't had it lately, with Millie watching her weight again.

"Who do you reckon we should see first, Guv?" he inquired, after a satisfying draught of beer.

"Young Henry, I think. We've something on him now."

"Then Miss Pendrick?"

Webb grinned and sliced into his quiche. "Down, lad, you're out of your depth! Yes, we'll have to see her. There are several points to clear up."

"Such as?" asked Jackson, with his mouth full.

"First, why she was more upset than her family expected. And secondly why she was frightened. Remember almost the first thing she said? 'Have they got him?' Not, 'Who did it?', mind. If she knows who the killer is, she might think she's next on the list."

"A lot to read into one remark, isn't it?"

"Maybe. And there was something else

which made me wonder. I asked when she last spoke to Mrs. Pendrick, and she replied, 'I didn't see her after Monday evening.' Anything strike you, Watson?"

"That she might have *spoken* to her later?"

"Exactly. Over the phone, for instance. Suppose she rang Nancy in London, and that was why she came dashing back?"

"But she didn't go to Frecklemarsh. As far as we know, she didn't contact her family at all."

"As far as we know. I might be on the wrong track, but a few more words with Miss Rose won't go amiss—you'll be glad to hear."

The housekeeper answered their knock. "Mr. Pendrick's at the hotel, sir," she informed Webb.

"It's young Mr. Pendrick we'd like to see. Is he in?"

"Yes, sir. If you'll wait in the sitting-room, I'll ask him to come down."

The Christmas tree was still there, its branches barer than on their last visit. "I wish someone would take it down," Webb said irritably. "Hasn't anyone here heard of Twelfth Night?"

Jackson regarded it sombrely. "Mrs. Pendrick probably put it up. Never thought it'd last longer than she did."

They turned as Henry Pendrick came into the room. His face was flushed and there was an air of defiance about him. Henny-Penny, thought Webb with sour humour.

"Sit down, Mr. Pendrick. There are a few points we'd like to go over. Wednesday afternoon, for instance. Where did you say you were?"

The boy swallowed nervously. "At the hotel."

"All afternoon?"

His tongue flicked out and was gone. "I think so."

"Think again, Mr. Pendrick. You were seen in Shillingham at five o'clock."

Henry's face flamed and his eyes moved rapidly from side to side. "Oh," he said weakly after a minute, "was—was that Wednesday?"

"What were you doing there?"

"It was—a private matter."

"I can't of course force you to tell me, but if you refuse it won't look good."

That startled him. "You don't think—I

157

mean, you can't imagine it had anything to do with—"

"You'd consulted your stepmother about something, hadn't you, sir? Something you didn't want her to talk about?"

He didn't reply. His hands were clasped tightly together.

"I wonder," Webb continued smoothly, "if your troubles stem from a gentleman called Lingford?"

Henry stared at him. "How the hell do you know about Robert?"

"Will you answer my question, please?"

"All right, if you must know I owed some money."

"Which you tried to borrow from your stepmother?"

Indignation made him incautious. "She was just being bloody-minded. There was no reason why I shouldn't have it—she was going to leave it to me anyway."

Webb watched with detachment as Henry realized with horror what he'd said. From being flushed, his face turned sickly white.

"But I didn't *kill* her—you can't think that! God, it was only a few hundred—not worth *killing* for!"

"People have been killed for much less."

"But I—"

"Suppose you tell us why you were in Shillingham."

His defiance had evaporated. "I took in some things to hock."

"What things?"

"Oh don't worry, they were mine. My video and a portable TV."

"You're in the habit of dealing with pawnbrokers?"

"No, but—"

"Mr. Lingford was able to advise you?"

Henry nodded miserably.

"Did you see anyone you knew there?"

"No, and I didn't think anyone saw me. Who was it?"

Webb ignored the question. "I'd like a complete account of your movements, please, and the exact time you arrived and left town."

"I left the hotel at five to four. It was ten past when I clocked into the car park."

"Which car park was that?"

"The station one. It was the nearest to where I was going."

It would be, Webb thought. Moneylenders, pawnbrokers—Station Road was the place to find them. "Go on."

"I went to the man Robert told me about and left the things. He didn't give me as much as I'd expected, but it was just about enough. Then I went round the corner to Boots. I spent some time looking at records, then I went on to Payne's and bought some shoes in the sale. I got back to the car at five past five. I know that, because I just got away with the minimum charge."

"And you drove straight home?"

"Yes."

"Mr. Pendrick, anything you say will be treated in confidence. Can you think of anyone at all who might have wanted your stepmother dead?"

"No, I can't. Nancy was the kind of person who infuriated you, but not the kind you *killed*."

"Someone did. If I asked you to describe her in one word, what would it be?"

Henry thought for a moment. "Super-efficient. Or is that two?" He reverted to more pressing matters. "Will Dad have to know about the video? He gave it me for my birthday."

"It's not our concern, but I'd advise you to confide in him. I'm sure he'd help."

"He'd throw the book at me."

"Perhaps you deserve it, but I think he'd sort things out. Very well, that's all for the moment. Could we have a word with your sister, please?"

"I'll see if I can find her."

"Bloody young fool!" Jackson said. "If he was mine, I'd give him a hiding."

"It's an illness, Ken, when it gets hold of you. Lingford's the one I'd like to get my hands on."

They waited several minutes, then Mrs. Foldes appeared in the archway. From her expression, Webb guessed she was an unwilling messenger.

"Miss Rose is using the sunlamp, sir. Would you like to go up?"

Jackson made a sound which he turned into a cough.

Webb said pleasantly, "Thank you, Mrs. Foldes, but it would be more convenient down here. We won't keep her long."

"Yes, sir." The woman looked relieved.

It was another five minutes before Rose joined them. She came barefoot, her robe tied loosely at the waist. Jackson guessed she'd nothing on under it, and the back of his neck grew hot. Forward minx, but God, she was gorgeous.

She settled herself on the sofa, legs tucked under her. Her skin was glowing from the lamp, her hair slightly tousled. In all, she looked as though she'd just left a lover's bed. But overriding this impression was a tenseness she couldn't conceal.

"How can I help you, Chief Inspector?"

"We hoped," Webb said steadily, "that you might have remembered something."

"Nothing at all." She held his gaze and despite himself, his pulse quickened. Come, come! he thought with amused impatience. Can't go lusting after the suspects!

"Such as, for instance, a phone call to London?"

The shot went home, he was sure of it. There was a second's stillness, then, control regained, she said lightly, "To Nancy, you mean? Now why on earth should I do that?"

"I don't know, Miss Pendrick. I hoped you'd tell me."

"We weren't on such cosy terms. I thought you knew that." She pushed back her hair and the movement loosened the robe, exposing a smooth mound of breast.

Webb said sharply, "Fasten your gown, please."

Smilingly she did so. "Doesn't the Bible say not to hide one's light under a bushel?"

Thank God for Ken! Webb thought with unaccustomed fervour. This one's a man-eater!

"Are you saying categorically that you did *not* phone Mrs. Pendrick last week?"

"I am."

"Then did she phone you, or anyone here?"

"Not as far as I know."

Liar! Webb thought, but outwardly he accepted it. "One last question, Miss Pendrick. What struck you most about your stepmother?"

"Her bossiness," Rose answered promptly. "She was always telling people what to do."

"Thank you, that's all. Sorry to interrupt your sunbathing."

"Any time, Chief Inspector."

Out on the path, Jackson sucked in his breath. "Know what I'd like for my birthday, all tied up in pink ribbon?"

"It was overdone, Ken. Didn't you feel that? She was laying it on to distract us. And damn near succeeding!" he admitted with a grin.

"If she was like that downstairs, just imagine if we'd gone to her room!"

"Stop imagining, lad. I need your full attention. We are now going to The Gables to inquire of Monsieur whatever his name is why he confirmed Henry's story of being in the kitchens. And he'd better have a damn good explanation, or in my present mood, I'll clap him in irons for obstruction."

9

THE receptionist looked up as they walked into the hall. It wasn't the girl they'd seen previously.

"Good afternoon, can I help you?"

Webb produced his card. "We'd like a word with one of your chefs, please. Monsieur—Bouvier, is it?"

"Yes, of course. Would you like to go to the kitchen, or shall I send for him?"

Webb glanced round the reception area and the lounge beyond. It was deserted. "It would be easier to talk here."

"Certainly. I won't keep you a moment."

Jackson looked about him. The hotel was furnished like a country house. There were landscape paintings on the walls and the furniture, though elegant and decorative, looked comfortable. "Plush, isn't it?" he said.

"It should be. People think nothing of driving out from London, never mind Bath or Gloucester, for the pleasure of eating here. The M4 upset the farmers, but it was the making of this place."

The pastry chef was coming warily towards them. He was a small man and to Jackson seemed typically French. He had dark hair, mostly hidden under his tall hat, large brown eyes like an unhappy spaniel and a comically drooping moustache. Had he been playing the part on stage, he couldn't have been more in character.

"Messieurs?"

"Good afternoon, Chef. There's a point in your statement we'd like to check, please. You informed us that Mr. Henry Pendrick spent Wednesday afternoon under your supervision."

"*Oui*. That is correct."

"The whole afternoon?"

"Not entirely, monsieur. He was for a while with his father." The chef had the usual Gallic difficulty with his "th".

"His father?" Webb frowned. "Are you sure?"

A shrug. "Well, monsieur, I assumed—"

"Why did you assume, Chef?"

"Because Monsieur Henri tell me he go

166

out for a while. And when later I go to speak wiz Monsieur Pendrick, he is not there. Two, three times I return and still his office is empty. So I assume he is gone out with Monsieur Henri."

"You're saying," Webb said slowly, "that Mr. Pendrick senior was not in his office on Wednesday afternoon?"

"Oh, assuredly he was there at one time. But not, as you say, the *'ole* afternoon."

"What time was it that you looked for him?"

Bouvier raised his shoulders. "At five, again at the quarter, and at almost six o'clock."

"I see. And when did Mr. Henry Pendrick leave you?"

"At four, I think. He had done what was required. I did not expect his return."

"Thank you, Chef. You've been very helpful."

"De rien, monsieur."

He walked quickly away and Webb and Jackson followed more slowly.

"We'll have a word with Mr. Pendrick now," Webb told the receptionist.

"Shall I see—?"

"Never mind, we know the way."

167

The door was heavy, of polished mahogany. Webb knocked firmly and Pendrick's voice called, "Come." Jackson grinned to himself and followed his superior into the room. It was large and attractively decorated, more like a study than an office, with easy chairs and a drinks cabinet. During the interviews on Saturday, the Governor had been behind the desk. Now, Pendrick was seated there, but he rose as they went in. He did not look pleased to see them.

"Good afternoon, gentlemen. Any news?"

"Nothing concrete as yet, sir. In the meantime, I've a few more questions."

"You'd better sit down, then."

Webb settled himself in a chair and regarded the man behind the desk. "Mr. Pendrick, as you'll appreciate, the most important person in this inquiry is the victim. We need to know all we can about her—her likes and dislikes, her virtues and vices—everything that will throw any light on her character. The more we know about her, the more chance we have of finding her killer."

Pendrick spread his hands. "Naturally I'll help all I can."

Webb asked his question for the fourth time. "What would you say was your wife's outstanding characteristic?"

He thought for a moment. "Her independence, I suppose. I certainly underestimated it."

"How was that, sir?"

Pendrick clasped his hands on the desk. "I don't know what you've been told about my marriage, Chief Inspector, but the truth is that although I was fond of my wife, and am naturally appalled at what's happened, our marrying was a mistake."

Now we're getting there, Webb thought.

"When we met I was very lonely, and since she was divorced and living alone, I thought she was, too. I was wrong. I also assumed we'd an interest in common. Wrong again. She didn't want to hear about the hotel, or my hopes for it. All that concerned her were Dean Catering and the school. They were her babies, and she'd no time for anyone else's."

"Does that include your son and daughter?"

"I was speaking metaphorically, but it does. She made no attempt to be a mother —insisted they call her by her first name, and so on. Of course, they were almost grown-up—sixteen and nineteen at the time, and they resented her. It wasn't easy for Nancy, either."

"When did you realize your marriage was a mistake?"

"When she made it clear she wouldn't live with me." He laughed harshly. "And I was marrying for companionship? Pathetic, isn't it? But I'd proposed and she'd accepted. It only emerged later that she meant to spend half her time in London. I should have finished it then, but by that time—well, we'd spent weekends together, and so on and I felt I couldn't back down. And at first it was a more reasonable division. She was here Friday afternoon to Monday lunch-time. But it gradually shrank and shrank till I wondered why she bothered coming at all."

"Which was the cause of the argument at New Year?"

"Yes."

Webb said casually, "Where were you on Wednesday afternoon, sir?"

There was a fractional pause and Pendrick's fingers, playing with a pencil, stilled. "I told you. I was here, working."

"Not, I think, the entire afternoon."

A longer pause, which Webb finally broke. "I'm sure you realize, sir, that this question is crucial to our inquiries?"

Oliver Pendrick spoke quietly. "Yes, I do realize, and I'm extremely sorry, but I can't answer it."

Jackson looked up from his notebook, blue eyes suddenly alert.

"I'd advise you, sir, to consider very carefully. We've established that you were absent from your office from at least five o'clock until after six. Possibly a margin on either side. That coincides very closely with the time of your wife's death."

Pendrick had gone pale, but his eyes held Webb's steadily. He made no reply.

"I put it to you again, sir. Where were you between those times?"

"I'm sorry, I can't tell you."

"You mean you refuse to?"

"Regretfully, yes."

"Very well. It's your right, of course."

He paused. "To go back a bit, I believe your first wife also died tragically?"

Pendrick's mouth twisted. "Tactfully put, but I get your drift. To paraphrase Wilde, losing one wife may be regarded as unfortunate; to lose two smacks of carelessness."

"She was killed in a fall, I believe?"

"Correct. She fell downstairs and died instantly."

"Were you in the house at the time?"

The old bugger! Jackson thought admiringly. He'd gone over the case with DCI McLean, now retired, and read all the reports. There wasn't much he didn't know about it.

Pendrick answered him steadily. "I was. In bed, as a matter of fact. My wife was late home."

"You were asleep?"

"No, I never slept till she came in."

So she made a habit of going out, Jackson noted.

"Where had she been, sir?"

His mouth twitched. "To dinner with friends."

Jackson felt a surge of sympathy. Poor devil, the memory of that death hurt more

172

than the recent one. He *could* have pushed her: the police were suspicious at the time, but then we're a suspicious lot. And according to the inquest, she was pooped to the eyeballs.

"Did you see her fall?"

The pencil snapped between Pendrick's fingers. In the still room, the crack sounded very loud. He sat staring at the two pieces. Then he laid them neatly side by side on the blotter, and looked up. A nerve twitched at the corner of his eye.

"Yes, I did. I heard a sound and opened the bedroom door. As you know, it's at the top of the stairs. Our eyes met briefly, then she teetered and fell backwards. Don't you think I've asked myself time and again whether my opening the door startled her, made her lose her balance? I'll live with that possibility for the rest of my life."

Webb cleared his throat. "Your car's been returned from Forensic, I believe?"

"It has."

"Can you explain the presence of a dark, female hair on the passenger seat?"

Pendrick stared at him. Possibly the abrupt switch of topic confused him. Then he said quietly, "I often give people lifts, Chief Inspector; several of them ladies with dark hair."

"Could I have their names, please?"

The question seemed to throw him. After a moment, he said haltingly, "Mrs. Bartlett, Mrs. Piper—"

"Mrs. Frayne?"

He said stiffly, "I've never given Mrs. Frayne a lift."

It would be easy to check. "I believe, sir, that you and she were once engaged?"

"My word, Chief Inspector, your bloodhounds have been busy! I wonder what other useless information they've unearthed."

"You deny it?"

"Of course I don't deny it, man. It's common knowledge. The point is, I treated Mrs. Frayne—or Miss Jarvis, as she then was—very badly in the past, and have the grace to be ashamed of it. That being so, I don't go out of my way to seek her company."

"She was at your party."

"Nancy's doing rather than mine. She insisted we couldn't invite the Cudlips without the Fraynes."

"How long have Dr. and Mrs. Frayne been here?"

"About six weeks, I suppose."

"Did you know before they arrived who Mrs. Frayne was?"

"No. Mrs. Bartlett met her in the village. She came and told me."

"And you told your wife?"

"Of course. If I hadn't, somebody else would have done."

"How did you feel about her living locally?"

"Embarrassed, frankly. As I say, I'd behaved badly."

"And you'd not met till your wife asked her to the party?"

"No."

"Mrs. Pendrick had no qualms about the invitation?"

"Of course not. She wasn't given to petty jealousies."

"And you still can't inform us of your movements on the afternoon of the fourth?"

"No." No regret this time. Webb accepted that he'd forfeited the right to it.

"Very well, Mr. Pendrick. We won't take up any more of your time."

Pendrick hesitated, curiosity over-coming his hostility. "Did you have any luck tracing Dean?"

"No, sir. He was staying in Shillingham, but he's left now."

Pendrick rose slowly to his feet. "When did he leave?"

"Last Wednesday. A lot going on that day, wasn't there, sir, one way or the other?" And nodding pleasantly at Pendrick, he left the room, Jackson at his heels.

Rose lay full length on the sofa, eating an apple. She was still in her bathrobe and the sash had loosened again, which was causing a degree of agitation to the young man perched on the arm. To disguise it, he said lightly, "So you've been grilled by the Fuzz? How very entertaining."

Henry said shortly, "They knew all about you."

"My life's an open book, Henny, as well you know."

"Don't call me that."

"Sorry. Old habits die hard." He drew on his cigarette. "What were they like, these arms of the law?"

Rose's small teeth crunched into the apple and the juice spurted on her chin. She wiped it away, gazing down the length of the sofa at Robert Lingford. Damn it, he thought angrily, she knows bloody well the effect she's having.

"Actually," she said, "the Chief Inspector's rather dishy."

"A bit uncouth," Henry protested.

"That, brother dear, is part of his charm. Gamekeepers are thin on the ground this season."

"She's going through one of her slumming phases," Henry told his friend. "You should have seen—"

Rose swung her feet to the floor and sat up quickly. "Robert darling, pass me another apple—they're in the bowl behind you. You didn't tell me the police mentioned Robert, Henry. What's he been up to?"

"Nothing, I swear." Lingford tossed her an apple. "It's Henry—*Henry*—who nearly got nabbed, but thanks to my good offices he's in the clear."

"Oh Henry, you're not *still* gambling?"

"I won almost a grand," he said defiantly.

177

"And lost it—and more—the next week."

"Henry, you *didn't*! However will you manage?"

He said unwillingly, "I've hocked some things, my video among them."

"Does Father know?"

"Not yet."

"He'll be livid."

Henry'd had enough of the conversation. "How about a round of golf, Robert? I'm not on duty till eight. Front of the house tonight."

"If you like." Lingford's eyes were still on Rose.

"I'll go and change. Shan't be a tick." Brightening visibly, Henry hurried from the room and Lingford slid down to the sofa beside Rose.

"How about being kind to an old friend?"

"Don't be silly, Robert."

The bloom on her averted cheek, the faint perfume of her skin, started his heart pounding. He put an arm round her but she resisted. "I've told you before, you're like my brother. I've known you all my life."

178

"I don't feel like a brother, believe me."

She looked into his eyes and smiled slowly. "You're supposed to be playing with Henry, not me."

"God, Rose, if there's a chance—"

"There isn't. At least—" it was amusing to keep him dangling—"not at the moment. I'll think about it." His eyes were close together, she reflected dispassionately, and his hands clammy. The thought of them on her body was displeasing. The Chief Inspector, now, was another matter, and she'd caught the leap of awareness in his eyes before officialdom closed down. If she could get rid of the little Sergeant, she might be in with a chance.

The idea excited her. Young men were so boring, like over-sexed puppies, whereas someone older—

Unwelcome memories swamped her without warning. Scarcely knowing what she did, she pulled the startled Robert against her, savaging his mouth with hers. Concentrate on this—and this—and this. Don't, for God's sake, think of anything else.

Henry's voice reached them, calling to

Mrs. Foldes. "I'm off for a round of golf now. Tell Dad I'll be over by eight."

Rose pushed Robert away and stumbled to the window. Before he could follow her, Henry'd arrived.

"OK, my clubs are in the hall . . . Robert?"

"Yes. Yes, I'm coming."

He was waiting for her to turn. She stood motionless, gazing out at the frost-lit garden where blackbirds hopped on the crisp grass.

"See you, Rosie."

"See you," she repeated woodenly.

Robert said hoarsely, "Goodbye, Rose."

She didn't reply.

10

IT was ten o'clock on the Wednesday morning, and the daily briefing was in progress. Webb looked at the circle of expectant faces. "OK, what have we got? You first, Alan."

Inspector Crombie studied the sheet in front of him. "Dick confirmed that your's and the victim's were the only prints on the diary. It and the address book have gone to Hampstead and they're following them up. It'll take time but there's no joy so far."

"Nothing on Dean yet, I suppose?"

"You'll be the first to know," Crombie promised drily.

Webb grunted and turned to Sergeant Partridge. "Don?"

"Nearly all the guests at the party have been seen, Guv. You asked us to leave you the Fraynes and Bartletts."

"Yes, I'll get along to them today. What of the others?"

"Not much help. The youngsters—

friends of the son and daughter—didn't take any notice of the older guests except when Dr. Frayne passed out. After them, we tried the Pipers. They live in the big farm at the foot of the hill."

"Has she got dark hair?" Webb interrupted.

Partridge looked surprised. "Yes, Guv. Going grey, as you might say. Pleasant lady, but she couldn't help. Didn't see or hear anything suspicious."

"Right." Webb turned to Dawson, who sat pulling at his lip. A tall, laconic man, the only time he'd been known to show emotion was at football matches.

"Bob? You and young Cummings have any luck?"

"Not with the Cudlips. They weren't pleased we knew about Dr. Frayne blotting his copybook. Played it down all they could and didn't volunteer much else. But we did better with the Grants; he was one of the gentlemen that took Frayne home." Dawson regarded Webb from under thick eyebrows. "He was looking for Mrs. Frayne, and guess where he found her? In the kitchen, with Mr. Pendrick."

182

Webb pursed his lips. "Now, that *is* interesting."

"He didn't think anything of it, so I didn't press it. No point in stirring things up."

"So for a while at least they were alone, which certainly wasn't the impression Pendrick gave."

"Could have wanted shot of his wife after all."

"Then he'll have to go after the doctor next! No," Webb shook his head. "If Pendrick's the one, the motive won't be that simple. She'd probably have given him a divorce, if he'd asked her. I'm beginning to think she died because of what she was."

"And what was she?"

"As always, different things to different people. Honest, efficient, bossy, independent. Since they're not incompatible, they could all be true. Which of those qualities could have led to her death? If we could only find out why she came back!"

"To speak to Dean?" hazarded Jackson.

"But what about, Ken? And why not wait till the weekend?"

Marshbanks leant forward eagerly. "We

183

know she phoned him, sir, but he could have rung her earlier. Or written, asking her to contact him."

"If he'd intended killing her," Partridge objected, "he wouldn't have arranged to meet her at his digs, with the landlady there and all."

"But perhaps he *didn't* intend to kill her. Perhaps everything went wrong."

"Go on, lad," Webb instructed.

"Well, sir, I was just thinking that if he *had* wanted to kill her, surely he'd have gone to London, rather than bring her back here. I mean, it would be much harder to pin it on him there, wouldn't it?"

"It's not so bloody easy here!" Dawson muttered under his breath. But the Governor was eyeing young Simon approvingly. A bit of initiative went a long way with Spiderman.

"That's an interesting theory, lad. She told them at the catering firm something important had come up. Presumably it concerned Dean. He could have been in trouble again, and wanted her help."

"If so, he didn't get it," Jackson

commented. "Mrs. Tallow heard them yelling at each other."

"Like the Constable said, perhaps things didn't go according to plan."

"Turning round Simon's idea," Crombie suggested, "suppose the killer was someone she knew in London? He could have followed her here to make it seem a local killing."

"Meaning it had nothing to do with Dean? Then why did he scarper?" Partridge shook his head. "My money's on him. Ex-husbands are a dodgy lot when it comes to murder."

"So are present husbands," Webb reminded him, "and this one's mighty secretive about his doings at the time. However, after what Bob's just told us, I reckon he was probably whooping it up with his old flame, rather than strangling his wife."

He stood up and stretched. "OK, that's all for now. Keep plugging away, lads. Ken, you and I'll go back to Frecklemarsh. I want a look at the doctor's wife."

Heather Frayne said steadily, "There's

very little I can tell you. That was the only time I met Mrs. Pendrick."

"But you knew her husband, I think?"

She bent her head and loops of dark hair hid her face. "A long time ago, yes."

"There'd been no contact between you in the meantime?"

"None at all."

"And you were quite happy to come and live in the same village?"

She hesitated, then said candidly, "Not happy exactly, no. I was rather apprehensive, but my husband wanted to be near his mother. This post was advertised, so naturally he applied."

"Have you any children, Mrs. Frayne?"

"One daughter, yes."

"Does she know the young Pendricks?"

"No. None of us had met till that weekend."

"And she wasn't asked to the party?"

"She was spending the New Year in Ripon."

"Where were you, last Wednesday afternoon?"

Her head reared and her startled eyes met Webb's. "Here. At home."

"Was your daughter with you?"

"No, she didn't come back till Thursday."

"And your husband?"

"He had hospital visiting, then evening surgery."

"So you were alone from when?"

She moistened her lips. "From lunch-time till about seven."

"And you remained here the whole time?"

Her hands were twisting in her lap. "I did go out to post a letter."

"Did you meet anyone?"

She shook her head, not looking at him. She's hiding something, Jackson thought. Don't say *she* went to Shillingham, too!

"Will your husband still be at the surgery, Mrs. Frayne?"

She glanced at the clock. "No, he'll be on his rounds now."

"When do you expect him home?"

"About twelve-thirty, for lunch."

"We'll call back then, if we may, to have a word. Won't hold you up more than we have to."

Heather watched them walk down the path, the lanky Chief Inspector and the smaller, slighter Sergeant. It was so *unfair*!

she thought hotly. All hope of keeping her connection with Oliver private had been thrown to the winds, just because—

She closed her eyes, checking the thought. *Just because Nancy was murdered.* How selfish could she get? Poor Nancy, lying in some horrible place unable even to be buried, and she complained about answering a few questions. She was ashamed—and for more reasons than one.

She turned swiftly from the window and with shaking hands resumed her interrupted housework.

Patty Bartlett greeted them pleasantly. She was a tall, attractive woman—dark-haired, certainly, and with large brown eyes that surveyed them with quiet concern. "Would you like a coffee, Chief Inspector? It must be cold work, trailing round asking questions."

"That's very kind of you, ma'am. Thank you."

It was an interesting house, but not the sort that appealed to Jackson, very modern, with lots of huge plate-glass windows. Like living in a ruddy goldfish bowl. Still, he supposed it was what you'd expect if you married an architect.

"You're old friends of the Pendricks, I believe," Webb began, stirring his coffee.

"Of Oliver, yes. And, of course, poor Avis."

"Did you think his second marriage was happy?"

"No," she answered quietly, "though he never hinted as much. But Nancy wasn't right for him. For a start, she was never here."

"You expected them for dinner last Friday?"

"That's right; Oliver came alone. He said Nancy'd phoned her apologies and would try to come later." She paused. "Obviously that wasn't true."

"Why do you think he said it?"

"Because he felt let down and didn't want to admit he hadn't heard from her. Though as it turned out, it wasn't her fault, poor girl."

"Did you like her as a person?"

"Oh, she was pleasant enough, but I couldn't relax with her. She'd far too much energy; you could feel it pent up

189

inside her, as though it was an effort for her to sit still."

"Did you notice any kind of tension at the party?"

"Not really. There was the usual false bonhomie you get at New Year, everyone being excessively friendly. A kind of insurance, I always feel. But tension—no, I wouldn't say so."

"And on Friday, here. How did Mr. Pendrick seem then?"

"Unhappy. He was making an effort, but we know him too well to be deceived."

"I hear it was you who told him about Mrs. Frayne." She nodded. "How did he react?"

She smiled reflectively. "He said, 'My God, as if I haven't enough on my plate!'"

"What do you suppose he meant?"

"Oh, Rose was being difficult, and there'd been some trouble at the hotel. A barman caught pilfering."

"Would you say he was worried at the prospect of meeting Mrs. Frayne?"

"Not particularly. He could have done without it, that's all."

"He didn't give any sign of still being fond of her?"

Patty Bartlett opened her big brown eyes. "After twenty-five years and two marriages? Good heavens no!"

"And when they met at the party, was there any awkwardness between them?"

"No, they carried it off very well."

"Did it occur to you that Dr. Frayne's drinking might have something to do with his wife?"

"No, it certainly didn't." She plainly found the question distasteful, and her easy cooperation dissolved. Webb sighed. Still, he'd had to ask. And she'd given him all she could.

"Is your husband home, Mrs. Bartlett?" There'd been two cars in the drive.

"Yes, he's working in the studio. Would you like to speak to him?"

"If we may."

She went into the hall, calling up the open stairway, "Jeff? Could you come down a minute?"

But Jeff Bartlett, casual in sweater and jeans, could add nothing to his wife's account. It seemed to Webb that, though shocked by Nancy's murder, the Bartletts didn't mourn her personally.

Nor was the return visit to the Fraynes any more helpful. His wife stayed in the kitchen while the doctor answered Webb's questions in a series of monosyllables. He was a loosely-knit man with thick wavy hair and a discontented mouth. Unable to keep still, he was continually crossing and uncrossing his legs, feeling in his pockets, drumming his fingers on the arm of his chair.

"Did you have any reservations, Doctor, about moving so near to your wife's ex-fiancé?"

"Why the hell should I?"

"You knew she was reluctant to come here."

"You can't spend your life avoiding people."

"And you've had no reason to regret your decision?"

Peter Frayne uncrossed his legs and frowned. "What are you getting at?"

Webb said smoothly, "Just that the murder must be a strain on her."

"I don't see why. I mean, we're sorry,

and all that, but it's not as though Mrs. Pendrick was a friend."

Webb looked at him thoughtfully. Had he consciously closed his mind to Pendrick's sudden availability, or had it simply not occurred to him?

Frayne glanced impatiently at his watch. "At the risk of seeming rude, I've a limited lunch-hour. There are a lot of calls still to make, so if that's all—?"

"Yes, Dr. Frayne," Webb said heavily, "that's all."

"So there we are," he commented, as Jackson drove up the hill out of Frecklemarsh. "Any ideas you'd like to kick around?"

"Only that I wouldn't let Frayne treat my tortoise!"

"My feelings exactly. I shouldn't be surprised if he's hitting the bottle fairly regularly. OK, Ken, back to Carrington Street to write up this lot, then we've the reconstruction at four-fifteen."

As always, it gave Webb an eerie feeling to see the woman police officer dressed in the victim's clothes. With her red hair bundled under a curly brown wig, Sally

Pierce bore an uncanny resemblance to Nancy Pendrick.

Preceded by television cameras, she turned out of Mrs. Tallow's path and made her way to Station Road. Sharon had refused to repeat her actions of the previous week, and another child took her place. Acting on instructions, she duly fell over and was helped up by Sally who, after a brief conversation, continued in the direction of Gloucester Circus. When she reached the corner, the exercise was abandoned. No one knew where Nancy had gone from there, nor how she'd been transported from the busy thoroughfare to the loneliness of Chedbury Woods.

A crowd had gathered to watch the re-enactment. Webb could only hope someone's memory had been jogged.

And someone's had. An hour later, as he was clearing his desk for the night, there was a knock on the door and Constable Jones looked in. He was a pasty-faced man in his fifties, whose sparse hair was plastered against his head.

"Pussy Barlow's downstairs, Guv. He'd like a word." The man referred to, an ex-cat burglar, was Jones's regular informer.

194

"OK, Alf, I'll be right down." Webb glanced at Crombie and grimaced. "Don't happen to have a nosegay on you, or a pomander or some such?"

"Not even a can of air freshener. Sorry."

"Oh well, all in the line of duty. You go if you're ready, Alan. I'll fill you in in the morning."

Pussy was in an interview room, and his peculiar aroma reached Webb as he opened the door. He was a small man, bald as a billiard ball, and with a nutbrown wrinkled face. There wasn't a spare ounce of flesh on him, and his hands and feet were small and nimble. Looked in good trim, Webb thought sourly. Probably still in business.

"Hello, Pussy. What can we do for you?"

The man's shifty little eyes slid away from his. "Well, Mr. Webb, the boot's on the other foot, as you might say. Think I might have something to interest you, if the price is right."

Webb kept his voice level, but he felt a jerk of excitement. They were due for a break. "The price, Pussy, as you well

195

know, depends on the information. We'll decide what it's worth when we've heard it."

The man gave an exaggerated sigh. "You're a hard nut, Mr. Webb. All right, I'll trust you. I saw that bird last week. The one that got the chop."

"*When* did you see her, Pussy?"

"She was walking down Station Road, like. It was the kid brought it back. I was on the other side, waiting to cross over, when she come running out of an alley and cannons straight into this bird in the fur jacket. The woman bent down to talk to her, but after a minute the kid shook her off and went running on up the road."

"And what did the woman do?"

"Ah-hah!" Pussy tapped the side of his nose knowingly. "That's where you got it wrong, see. She didn't go on to the Circus, like the woman cop did. She turned into the jigger the kid had come out of." He stuck his hands in his pockets and waited expectantly.

"And then what happened?"

Pussy looked offended. "Well, I don't know, do I? Didn't hang around all bleeding day."

"So you didn't see her come out again?"

"Nah."

"Was there a man anywhere near her?"

"No, boss. Not a blooming soul."

"Which alley was this, Pussy?"

"Down the side of the Indian takeaway. Leads through to Carlton Road."

"You saw all this while you were waiting to cross the road?"

"Yup. It happened very quick."

"And when you'd crossed, did you look down the alley?"

"Nah. Wasn't interested, was I? Thought no more about it till I saw the charade you put on just now. Well, was it any help or wasn't it?"

"Yes, Pussy, I think it was, and we're grateful to you for coming. Constable Jones will see you're suitably rewarded."

Webb nodded at both men, then, leaving the interview room, took the stairs two at a time. In his office, he went to the street map on the wall and located the alleyway. As Pussy'd said, it was a short cut to Carlton Road, cutting out Gloucester Circus. But no one going to Duke Street car park would have turned down it. Had Nancy always intended to go down there, or was it because of something Sharon had said? It was clear the child had lied, or at least edited her statement. If she'd only gone to the Co-op, she wouldn't have been near the alley. So what was she doing there? Meeting a boyfriend her mother didn't know about? He'd have to see her again, and preferably without Mrs. Robinson in attendance.

In the meantime, it was nearly six and he'd had enough for one day. Sergeant Partridge was still in the general office, and Webb paused briefly. "Don, get on to Stonebridge, will you. I'd like the wheels put in motion for some info from British Telecom: did anyone from the hotel or Gables Lodge put a call through to Belsize Gardens on the third or fourth of January?"

"Right, Guv. Will do."

The rain had started again, and the wind was getting up, winding the flaps of Webb's raincoat round his legs as he opened the car door. Impossible to judge the value of Pussy's information, but at very least it opened a new direction for Nancy's doings. What did she want in Carlton Road? With East Parade, it contained the better-class shops and one or two cafés and restaurants. Perhaps she'd decided on tea before starting back to London? If so, it was the obvious place to head for.

Webb drove slowly out on to Duke Street and turned right, away from the town centre. Down this end, the road housed mainly offices, and a few late workers were queuing in the rain for buses. Waiting at the traffic lights, his memory played back the day just gone: the briefing session, with the information that Pendrick and La Frayne had been alone after all. Then the woman herself, quiet and tense, and her jumpy, inconsiderate husband. Suppose her return affected Pendrick more than they'd realized?

Pursuing his thoughts, Webb drove up the hill. The flats where he lived stood in the grounds of the gracious houses they'd replaced and still bore their names. He turned into the drive of Beechcroft Mansions, and went along it to the garage. On his left, the garden lay darkly in the wind and rain. No temptation tonight to linger with his sketch pad.

Spurning the lift, he went up two flights

of stairs, pausing briefly on the first landing to glance at Hannah's door. There'd been no contact between them since Saturday's questioning. Perhaps Miss Yates was still there.

His thought waves might have reached her, for ten minutes later Hannah knocked on his door. "Hello, David. How's it going?"

The reserve was still present. He stood to one side. "Come in. Is your aunt still with you!"

"No, she only stayed a couple of days. She had to prepare for the new term."

"I hope she wasn't too upset." It occurred to him that Charlotte Yates might be the only one who truly mourned Nancy.

A sizzling from the kitchen claimed his attention. "Excuse me—I left the chops on. Have you eaten?"

"No." She followed him. "I was going to ask you to join me, but I see I'm too late."

"Then let me do the honours. There's enough for two, and I often eat at your place."

"In that case, thank you. Anything I can do?"

"No, thanks." In his own way, he was quite an accomplished cook. When Susan left him, he'd vowed not to live out of tins.

Hannah sniffed the onion sauce appreciatively. "I seem to remember that the more involved you become in a case, the more elaborate your cooking."

He grinned, and his face was suddenly younger. "It's good therapy, I'll say that for it."

"*Have* you any leads, David?" She paused, then added: "You were right, I wasn't being helpful on Saturday. I was in a state of shock."

"I know." He turned the chops. "But it wasn't idle curiosity; I needed the answers. Fortunately your aunt supplied them."

"I thought she would, but I didn't want to forestall her. And I was afraid that what I said might be misleading, point to someone quite innocent."

"In fact, you didn't trust my judgement."

There was a silence, then Hannah said quietly, "It must have looked like that. I'm sorry."

"OK, no harm done." But he'd been hurt by her reticence and the fact annoyed him. "At least," he added wryly, "your aunt's interest in criminology can have full rein. Has she come up with any theories?"

"No, it's too close to home. She really was shaken, poor love. Being in Nancy's flat made it worse."

A gust of wind rattled the windows in a burst of rain. Hannah added, "I saw the reconstruction on the news. Is it likely to help, do you think?"

"We'll have to wait and see."

She gave a short laugh. "All right, I'll stop pumping you. But we are friends again, aren't we?"

He pulled her against him, resting his face on her hair. "Friends." His mood began to lighten. Hannah always had the knack of calming him down. Mentally, that is; physically it was the reverse, which was a combination he couldn't fault.

He tipped her head back and kissed her. "Now, if you don't stop distracting the cook, the meal won't be worth eating."

She laughed and turned away, beginning to lay the table. Tonight, he thought, they can go to hell, the lot of them: Oliver

Pendrick, his spoilt son, his sexy daughter, and the rest. Tomorrow they would again have his full attention, but they'd no claim on the hours between. Those belonged exclusively to him. And Hannah.

And, as always, they were restorative. Much later, as they lay together, calm and relaxed, Hannah said suddenly, "Well? Aren't you going to talk about the case?"

He turned, but the moonlight which filled the room left her face in shadow. "Now?"

"Oh come on, David, you always do. When we're lying quietly like this, you use me as your sounding-board."

It was true. Release of physical tension brought corresponding mental respite, and many of his problems, talked over in this dark and tranquil room, had effortlessly resolved themselves. He'd hoped Hannah wouldn't comment on the fact that tonight he'd remained silent.

She said softly, "You still haven't forgiven me, have you?"

"It's not that," he said awkwardly.

"I think it is. You feel I'm involved in

this case, even at a distance, so I can't be treated as an impartial audience."

He smiled in the darkness and his fingers caressed her shoulder. "Psychology you read at Oxford, was it?"

"It's obvious. But I still want to help, David. And as for repeating anything, even to Charlotte, this bed is like the confessional. You know that. Don't—shut me out."

He moved protestingly. "I'm not, love. Really. It's just that I'm not ready yet to sound out my ideas. Too many loose ends. Now, if you were to invite me back in two or three days, things might be different!"

"Always ready to assist the police," Hannah said demurely, and turned to meet his mouth.

11

"YOU'RE blinking cheerful this morning, aren't you, Guv?" Jackson said accusingly as they drove out of the police station.

Webb grinned. "Another day, another dollar. Something's got to break soon. Perhaps Pussy was the start of it. At any rate, I want a word with young Sharon on exactly what passed between her and Nancy. It's a point that's niggled me all along; she didn't repeat anything she'd said herself, yet according to her statement, Nancy said, 'Whatever's the matter?' and then, 'What happened?' Now, that's not what you'd say to a kid who's fallen over—it's perfectly obvious what's happened. But if, as Pussy said, she came rushing in a distressed condition from a dark passageway, then it's just the kind of thing you *would* say."

"And that could be why Mrs. P went down the alley," Jackson added. "I mean, if the kid had seen a mugging or a break-

205

in or something, she might have gone to deal with it, and got more than she bargained for."

"Except that no crimes were reported that day. Anyway, I want a good look at the alley myself as soon as we've finished here."

They had drawn up at 124 Wellington Street. The outer door was closed. "Looks as if no one's home. We'll ring the bell, anyway."

It was not answered, and they were still standing there when a woman turned in at the next gateway. "They're away," she told them over the dividing wall. "Doris's mother's been took bad. Won't be back till the weekend."

Webb thanked her and they got back into the car. "So we're stymied there, which is a nuisance. OK, Ken, let's look at that alley."

A delivery van was pulling out as they came down Station Road, and Jackson slipped into the gap. Directly alongside was the Punjabi Gardens, its interior hidden by red brocade curtains. A card on the door informed them it was open daily from six p.m. to midnight.

"We'll have to check, Ken, but it seems unlikely anyone'd be around at four-thirty, and if they were, they wouldn't see much from behind that lot. Is there a back entrance?"

"We can look from the alley."

The alley itself, some eight feet wide, stretched in front of them, hemmed in by high walls on either side. The building to the right was a betting shop, and the two policemen went inside. The proprietor, over-eager to help, had nothing to offer. He'd watched the reconstruction, but the preceding drama hadn't penetrated his painted windows.

Having expected nothing more, Webb and Jackson set off down the alley. Two women were coming along it, chatting animatedly, and the policemen pressed against the wall to let them pass. At intervals, gates had been let into the walls, but the majority were boarded up. Fish and chip papers, soaked with rain, had blown against them, and there was a prevailing smell of cats.

After about fifty yards a turning branched off to the right and the men followed it, emerging minutes later in a large, rectangular space. It was the Odeon car park. Across the wide expanse, they could see the traffic in Carlton Road.

"Beresford parked here that afternoon," Webb commented. "Pity he didn't come out earlier—he might have walked in on the action."

They retraced their steps and continued to the end of the alley, where they stood for a minute or two, watching the shoppers in Carlton Road. Then, in silence, they turned and walked back to the car.

"Pretty barren sort of place," Jackson ventured at last. "As far as I can see, it's a short cut and nothing else."

"True. So why did it prove fatal for Nancy Pendrick? If, indeed, it did: she might have emerged safely into Carlton Road and met her fate there. Or any other damn place, for all we know."

"Perhaps Dean saw her turn into the alley and went in after her. She was delayed by meeting Sharon; he could have caught up with her."

"It's possible. Make a U-turn here if you can, Ken. We'll go back and have a word with Mrs. Tallow. She might know whether Dean had a job, and if so, what it was."

Mrs. Tallow greeted them with her customary surliness, though an air of self-importance had crept in. Television cameras at her gate, despite the sordid reason for them, gave an improved standing with her neighbours.

"Of course he had a job," she said, in reply to Webb's query. "Wouldn't have taken him in without one—couldn't have paid the rent, could he? And I wouldn't want him mooching round here all day."

"Do you know where he worked?"

"The music shop in Birchall Place. I saw him one day, when I went to the market."

"Thanks very much, Mrs. Tallow. I suppose there's been no word from him?"

Her expressive sniff was answer enough.

"What puzzles me, Ken," Webb said as Jackson started the car, "is why he came to Shillingham when the hotel sacked him. Pendrick assumed he'd returned to the Smoke—said he was a born Londoner—and it can't have been Nancy who was the attraction; he'd have had more chance of seeing her in London."

A possible solution was offered at the music shop. It was a small, crowded place, with a stereo playing at full volume, and they had difficulty making themselves heard. But when the staff realized what Webb wanted, they were willing to talk of Dean.

"One for the girls, was old Danny," the manager said with a smile. "One of our young ladies was quite smitten, but though he played her along, he didn't ask her out. She was quite upset."

Webb was wondering if, thirty-odd years ago, he'd played his 78s at that volume. He doubted it; his father would have scalped him.

"But then he wouldn't, would he," the manager continued, "when he'd already got a girl. To hear him talk, you'd think she was a cross between Raquel Welch and Princess Di!"

"What was her name, did he say?"

"No, that's one thing he kept to himself."

"Did she ever come here?"

"I never saw her. She phoned once—or some bird did. Arranging to meet in the lunch-hour, I think."

"And he didn't leave a forwarding address?"

Some hope, thought Jackson, when he'd done in his wife!

"We didn't even know he was going. Wednesday morning he was as chirpy as usual. It was half-day closing, but there was no hint he wouldn't be back next day."

Which was what Mrs. Carstairs said about Nancy. Neither, that Wednesday morning, had foreseen anything unusual in their meeting, yet both had disappeared after it, Nancy to be found dead and Dean still missing. What the devil had it been about?

"This girlfriend of Dean's: did he show you a photo?"

"Yes he did, if it really was her. Looked a bit too classy in my opinion, but she was a cracker all right."

"Could you describe her, sir?"

The man shrugged. "The usual. Long legs, blonde—you know the type."

Jackson looked quickly at Webb, caught the sudden narrowing of his eyes. God, was it possible Rose Pendrick was involved with Dean? Was *that* why she'd been so frightened? They could have met while he was at the hotel, though why Rose should bother with the likes of Dean, he couldn't imagine.

"Back to Gables Lodge, I suppose?" he said, as they came out into the narrow confines of Birchall Place.

"Not yet, Ken. I want to wait till we get the gen on phone calls."

"So what now?"

"Mrs. Tallow again. Remember her saying 'It wasn't his usual girl'? I was concentrating on Nancy at the time and didn't pick that up. Let's see if her description tallies."

Heather opened the door and stood staring at him.

Oliver said, "I came to thank you for your letter."

"It was the least I could do." She hesitated. "Would you like to come in?"

"Thank you."

"You haven't met my daughter, have you? Joey, this is Mr. Pendrick."

A tall, dark girl unfolded herself from the sofa. She was wearing T-shirt and jeans and her hair fell in a straight sheet

212

down her back. She had her mother's eyes and her father's full mouth, softer and more appealing in its feminine form.

"My daughter, Joanna."

He took her long, narrow hand. "I'm sorry about your wife," she said.

"Thank you." Though the same age as Rose, she seemed both older and younger.

The girl glanced at her mother. "Shall I make some coffee?"

"Please, darling."

As the door closed behind her, Oliver said quietly, "I shouldn't have come, but I had to see you."

Heather's eyes moved over his face. "It's not very wise. If anyone—"

He said explosively, "God, Heather, how can all this have flared up in ten days?"

She moistened her lips. "I'm so very sorry—about Nancy."

"I presume the police have been?"

"Yes."

"Asking about Wednesday?" She nodded. "What did you say?"

"I didn't know what to say—or what you'd already told them."

"I kept your name out of it."

"I thought you would. I didn't mention you, either. I said I'd only been out to post a letter."

"And they believed you?"

"I don't know."

"They know I was out—God knows how—but I refused to say where."

"But Oliver, that's dangerous."

He shrugged. "They suspect the husband anyway. It's an occupational hazard."

"All the more reason to tell the truth."

"It's none of their damn business."

"But it is, in the circumstances." She shuddered. "You realize we were together at the exact time she was killed? It makes it all so much worse."

"Because she's dead?" His voice was harsh. "She wouldn't have cared if she were alive. And we weren't doing anything wrong, for God's sake, only driving round and round trying to sort things out."

"Then why not own up?"

"Because they wouldn't believe me. I know how their minds work."

"Darling, they're not interested in our morals. All they care about is whether one of us killed Nancy."

214

The door opened and Joanna reappeared with the tray. Oliver forced himself to sit back and relax. Her hair falling forward, Joanna poured the coffee and handed him a cup with a shy smile. A studious-looking girl; if he and Heather had married, she rather than Rose could have been his daughter. The two girls, each reminiscent of her mother at that age, brought back vividly the choice he'd made. Had it been the right one? If he'd married Heather as planned, both Avis and Nancy might be alive today. But to accept such a premise was to entrust the future to a toss of the dice.

He looked up to find the girl's serious eyes on him, and tried to rouse himself. "I hear you're off to college next week?"

"Yes, I'm studying medicine."

That at least he couldn't have bequeathed her, Oliver thought wryly. For several minutes they talked of medical matters, the prospects for qualified doctors, the pros and cons of emigrating. Speaking of her career, Joanna came warmly to life, her sallow face flushing with enthusiasm. He saw Heather's eyes, full of love, resting on her, and felt a stab of jealousy. For this wasn't his daughter, but Peter Frayne's.

The ringing of the phone interrupted them. Ignoring the instrument beside her, Joanna jumped up. "I'll take it upstairs," she said, and hurried from the room.

Oliver said, "I must go."

"Yes."

Heather rose with him. Impulsively he pulled her towards him and started to kiss her, feeling her ineffectual hands against his chest before, with a sound in her throat, she wound them round his neck. Almost at once she pulled away.

"This has got to stop. It's unfair to all of us."

"'All' including Peter?"

"Peter most of all. Don't look so stricken, darling, you know I'm right." She ran a finger gently over the bump on his nose.

He caught and held her hand. "Tell me the truth, Heather. Are you happy with him? If we hadn't met again, would you have been content to spend the rest of your life with him?"

"Of course," she said, surprised she didn't choke on the lie. He stared down at her, willing her to retract it, but it was the only lifeline she had, and she knew he would accept it.

"Very well," he said at last. "Then I've no right to complicate things."

"Joanna—" she began desperately.

"Yes. She needs a stable home with two loving parents. Which," he added bitterly, "is something my children never had." Nancy'd been right there. And though, heaven knew, she was rarely available, it was still to her rather than himself that Henry had turned with his problem. Now even that prop had gone, and he remembered Rose's disproportionate grief. How little he knew his son and daughter.

He said, "I wish I didn't feel so alone," and saw the pain in her face. God, what a mess he'd made of everything.

"Goodbye, Heather," he added, and before she could accompany him to the door, went quickly from the room and let himself out of the house.

It had started to snow, and, as if on cue, the central heating at the police station had broken down. Webb sat at his desk in his overcoat, sifting through reports sent by

217

the Hampstead police and rubbing his hands for warmth.

"Bloody marvellous, isn't it?" he said to Crombie. "The heat belts out full blast as long as the weather's mild, and it's like a greenhouse in here. But the minute we really need it, the damn thing goes off. Sod's law, I suppose."

"Anything of interest there?"

"No. She had a wide circle of friends, all of whom seemed fond of her. Quite a contrast to the impression we formed at Frecklemarsh."

"Any men among them?"

"Plenty, though all claiming to be platonic. I'm inclined to go along with that. I'd say Nancy was a woman who preferred men's company to women's, without any hint of sex coming into it. She was a strong character, self-willed, efficient, independent."

Crombie grinned. "If you're about to suggest those are male characteristics, watch it, or you'll be accused of chauvinism."

"What I'm getting at is that I doubt if her killing had a sexual motive."

"Still think it was linked with her character?"

"Yes. It could have been business rivalry, or something crooked she discovered and refused to keep quiet about. She wouldn't stand for anything shady."

"Which would suggest a London killer stalking her back here?"

"Perhaps. God, I wish we could catch up with Dean—he's delaying the whole shooting-match. Once we can either nail him or clear him, we'll have more to go on. He can't have disappeared into thin air."

"Unless," Crombie said slowly, "he's been murdered, too."

"God Almighty! I must say, Alan, you've a knack for cheering people up."

"Well, he could have been. Perhaps Nancy told him whatever it was she was on to."

"You know something? I wish to hell you'd never said that. Now we'll have to start a full-scale search—further into Chedbury Woods and thereafter in ever-increasing circles. There aren't any unidentified bodies lying conveniently in the mortuary, are there?"

"Not that I've heard, though I'll check."

"Well, get on to the Support Group. At least it'll give us a new direction to work in." He pushed his chair back, stuck his hands in his pockets and stood for a moment staring out of the window. A sheet of ice lay on the forecourt pond and large, fluffy flakes drifted steadily down, covering path and grass. Out in the road, traffic churned the whiteness to dirty slush, and the County Court opposite was veiled behind a dancing crystal curtain.

With a sigh, Webb turned up his coat collar. "'Once more unto the breach.' At least it'll be warmer out there!"

"I do wish the police would make a move," Mary Cudlip said, passing a dinner plate down the table. "It's like the sword of Damocles hanging over us. Imagine how Oliver must feel. Ivor saw him in the village today, and he looked dreadful."

Heather held her breath. Had Joey mentioned Oliver's visit to Peter? Appar-

220

ently not. Peter said idly, "I wonder if they suspect him?"

Mary made a sound of distress, but Ivor Cudlip pushed out his lower lip reflectively. "First choice, the husband, isn't it? They'll be watching him pretty carefully."

The cadences of his native Wales still lingered in his voice. He was a big, good-looking man in his sixties, silver-haired and red-faced, with bushy eyebrows and a genial smile. "Can't be easy for him."

"Especially," put in Peter, "since it's the second time it's happened." He gave a short laugh. "It looks, my love, as though you had a lucky escape, all those years ago!"

Heather's face flamed and Mary said stiffly, "That's not funny, Peter. The fact that Oliver's had two tragedies is no laughing matter."

"Provided they *were* tragedies, and not convenient 'accidents'."

"That's enough, boy. Give it a rest, will you? Oliver's our friend."

Peter emptied his glass. "No offence. I didn't realize everyone was so touchy."

Mary thought: Oh dear, why did Ivor take him on? For all his qualifications, he's no good with people. He rubs everyone the wrong way—and he's so offhand with his wife. Though they hadn't known of Heather and Oliver's romance—over before they came to Frecklemarsh—it would have made no difference. It was all in the past and Ivor would have foreseen no problems. Nor should there be any, Mary assured herself uneasily. All the same, Oliver was in a vulnerable state to meet an old love, and Heather was clearly on edge.

Ivor was saying, "That girl of yours ready for college, then?"

"Raring to go. I just hope she knows what she's in for. Work, work, and more work, and precious few thanks at the end of it."

Heather said quickly, "To hear Peter talk, you'd never guess medicine's his whole life. Joey has the same single-mind-edness."

"It's a tribute to you, boy, that she wants to follow in your footsteps. I admit I was disappointed, when neither of ours showed interest." Dr. Cudlip glanced at the sideboard, where two graduation photographs were displayed. "Still, they're

222

doing well in their own fields. I've nothing to complain of."

Heather thought: I wonder what he's doing now? Probably greeting people arriving for dinner and trying to ignore their curious glances. Still, the fact that the restaurant was always full would conceal the presence of sensation-seekers.

Did the police suspect Oliver? Ought she to tell that Chief Inspector he was with her? But they might not believe her—think she was trying to shield him.

Oh God, Ivor was filling Peter's glass again. *Please* don't let him get drunk. The Cudlips had overlooked one occasion but another might give them pause. It had been hard enough covering for him in Ripon; in a place this size, there was no room for secrets. And she couldn't bear it if they had to leave Frecklemarsh.

The unconscious thought prodded consciousness, and she paused to consider it. After Oliver's visit that morning, to move would surely be the wisest course.

She started, aware that Mary was addressing her. "I'm sorry, what did you say?"

"Are you free tomorrow, dear? There's

a whist drive in the church hall; it would be a chance for you to meet people."

"It's kind of you, Mary, but I'm afraid I can't. I'm having tea with Peter's mother."

"Another time, then. How is she, by the way? I know you were concerned about her."

It was Peter who answered. "She feels the cold, but won't use the central heating. Says it's extravagant, for God's sake. Spends her time crouching over one bar of the electric fire, and thinks she's economizing. I've told her if she goes on like that, the economies will be in vain, because she won't be here to enjoy them. We've asked her to move in with us, but she won't hear of it. Independent as they come. So we'll just have to go on worrying, till the warmer weather comes."

"It is a problem, I know. There are elderly people here who live the same way. Sooner or later, someone sends for Ivor, but it's often too late."

Heather's attention slipped away again. Ivor said he'd looked dreadful. That must have been just after he'd left her. *"I wish I didn't feel so alone."* God, hadn't he hurt her enough? If they'd kept in touch over the years, the memories might have washed harmlessly away. Instead, their meeting at New Year was the first since he'd broken their engagement. She'd loved him then and she accepted despairingly that she still did. But now she had Peter and Joey dependent on her. She couldn't treat them as Oliver had her.

The evening came to an end. The snow had frozen where it lay, crunching under their feet as they walked home. In a high, clear sky, a handful of stars glittered coldly.

"At least Mother saved you from a whist drive!" Peter commented with a laugh. "My God, life in the fast lane!"

"It was kind of Mary to invite me."

"But you'd have to be pretty desperate to go."

But I *am* desperate, she thought in anguish. And what *am* I expected to do, while you're out on calls or snoring in a chair? She felt trapped, imprisoned in a cage of ice. And Joey was going away. Life shouldn't come to a standstill at forty-five. What did the agony aunts advise—join a club? Here, in Frecklemarsh? A *whist* club, perhaps! Angry tears came to her eyes and she blinked them away.

The hall light was on, that in the sitting-room off. Joey had gone to bed.

Leaving Peter to lock up, Heather went upstairs. In a sheath of misery she washed, undressed, brushed her hair. Peter climbed into bed beside her, with the usual creaking of springs.

"'Night, love." He kissed her cheek, turned over, and was immediately asleep.

Heather lay on her back, silent tears streaming down her face. In his way, because he was weak, he needed her. But it was a selfish, one-way kind of need. He'd never tried to understand her, discover her interests, ask her opinion. She was his wife and she supposed he loved her, but she was allowed no say in their lives. The return to Frecklemarsh was a case in point. She'd tried to dissuade him, and he'd laughed at her. Well, he'd brought it on himself.

The last phrase sounded an alarm, alerting her to the way her mind was working. But why not? she thought, with heady defiance. If by some miracle Oliver loved her, she couldn't let him go a second time. That was too much to ask. And since by becoming his lover she'd be happier, more complete, then Peter and Joey would benefit too. It was cockeyed reasoning, but she desperately needed to believe it.

She thought back to the morning's meeting. That lie about her marriage would keep him away unless she rescinded it. Very well, she would do so. She had known at the time it was her lifeline. Now, quite deliberately, she prepared to jettison it. She would sink or swim with Oliver.

12

FAITH came quickly into the dining-room. "Is it in? The announcement?"

Roger looked up. "Yes, it's in." He drew a deep breath. "I'm not sure I believed it myself, till I saw it in *The Times*."

She took the paper from him and read the paragraph. "Mr. Justice Beresford. It sounds impressive, doesn't it? Well done, my dear. You've worked hard for this."

She sat down and poured some orange juice. "I shall enjoy being Lady Beresford."

Sir Roger and Lady Beresford. He remembered, years ago, telling Avis of his ambition. "Don't get pompous, will you, when you're a judge?" she'd said. "If you do, I shall come to court and make faces at you!" Inconceivable, then, to have imagined life without her. Inconceivable now . . .

The windows rattled in a gust of wind.

"I hope the weather improves," Faith commented. "I promised to help Phyllis exercise her hunters." She opened her own newspaper, unaware of her husband's distraction. "They're still running that beastly murder, I see. Thank God no one here knows we're connected with it."

. . . Mr. Justice Beresford. Perhaps, one day, Lord Justice . . .

"Oliver could have done it, you know . . . Roger!"

"I'm sorry, my dear, what did you say?"

"I said Oliver could have done it."

He lowered *The Times*, narrowly missing the marmalade. "Done what, dear?"

"Killed her, of course."

He stared at her, then laughed uncertainly.

"I'm quite serious. There was a most unpleasant atmosphere between them, we remarked on it at the time."

"But it couldn't possibly be Oliver. Whatever—"

"Well, who else, for heaven's sake? Who else could want her out of the way?"

"If you ask me, it was one of those

senseless killings which are never solved. A drunk—"

"At four-thirty in the afternoon?"

"My love, there are people who are drunk all day. Or perhaps a mugger—"

"No, Roger. I'm sorry, but I don't agree. First, a drunk or mugger would have robbed her, and secondly he'd have left her where she was—presumably somewhere in Shillingham, since she left her car there. But this killer took her five miles by car—there was no other way—and dumped her. Why?"

"I'd no idea you'd taken so much interest in it."

"I've no option—it's thrust at me every time I read a paper or turn on the news. I just wish they'd bury poor Nancy, and the case with her, and let the rest of us get on with our lives."

Roger said drily, "I wasn't aware it inconvenienced you."

"It's hanging over all of us, and I resent it. If you remember, I didn't want to trail over there in the first place. If I'd known this would happen, wild horses wouldn't have dragged me. It's all right for you;

murders are part of your day's work, but I find it most distasteful."

"I'm sorry, dear."

"Well, I shall just stop reading the papers till it's all over."

"That would be best, if it upsets you." Roger folded his napkin and got to his feet. "Have a good day, dear, and be careful with the horses. It's slippery underfoot."

She raised her cool cheek for his kiss. "Drinks with the Leslies at seven, remember."

At the door he looked back, but she'd already returned to her newspaper. So much for her resolve, he thought with a smile as, shrugging into his coat, he left the house for the eight-forty.

"Oliver?"

"Heather! What is it? Is something wrong?"

He heard the smile in her voice. "Why should anything be wrong?"

"I wasn't expecting to hear from you."

"That's what I want to talk to you about."

"You've changed your mind?"

She said hurriedly, "We can't talk over the phone. Could you meet me this afternoon? A cup of tea somewhere?"

"Of course. Where?"

"How about the Copper Kettle in Heatherton? It's across the square from Faversham's."

"I'll find it. About three-thirty?"

"That'll be fine."

She replaced the receiver and stood for a moment staring unseeingly across the road. There was no going back now. In six and a half hours she would have to explain, try to persuade him of her reasoning. Please let him understand.

The communication from Headquarters was on his desk when Webb arrived that morning. He tore it open and read it, still standing.

"I knew it!" he said with satisfaction. "It's the info from British Telecom. A call was made from Gables Lodge to Hampstead at nineteen forty-three on Tuesday the third of January. Duration eight minutes. I'm willing to bet that's what brought Nancy back."

Crombie nodded. "So you were right. What's the next move?"

"Find out who made it. My money's on Rose. At very least, it should tie up some loose ends. We're into the second week now—time we made a bit of progress."

"I wouldn't mind making progress there myself! How about me going to see Miss Pendrick?"

Webb snorted. "She'd eat you for breakfast! No, that young lady needs special handling, and I reckon I'm the one to do it."

Ignoring Crombie's ribald comment, Webb lifted his phone. "Ken? We've got the gen on the phone call. Time for some more questions."

The sunshine was already melting the snow as they drove through the country lanes. The sky was clear, and above the fields rooks circled and called, jagged black outlines against the blue. Briefly, Webb longed for his sketch-pad, but that would have to wait.

"Rose first?" Jackson queried, as they came down into Frecklemarsh.

"Yes, Rose first, if she's available. If

not, we'll start with one of the others, but I don't want her getting wind of it."

"She's already said it wasn't her."

"I don't believe her, but I could be wrong. There's plenty of choice: Pendrick, the boy, Mr. or Mrs. Beresford—even the housekeeper. Basically they're all possibilities."

"The time may tie it down. Pendrick and his son could have been at the hotel."

The Lodge gates were open, and Jackson turned into them. The church clock was striking ten. Its measured chimes reached them clearly over the cold, still air.

"Bet Her Ladyship's still in bed!" Jackson said with a grin.

But he was wrong. Rose herself flung open the door, but her smile faded when she saw who it was. "Oh—I was expecting someone else."

"Sorry about that, miss. Can you spare us a minute?"

"*Again?* For heaven's sake, I've told you all I know." There was unease beneath the assumed impatience.

"That's what we'd like to check, miss."

"Very well. Come in, then." She turned

from the door, leaving Jackson to close it behind them. The sound of a record-player reached them from upstairs. Something Henry hadn't yet flogged, apparently.

The two policemen followed Rose to the sitting-room. She walked to the fireplace and turned, one arm casually along the mantelpiece. It was a studiedly insolent pose, implying she could only spare them a minute.

"It's about that phone call," Webb said stolidly.

Her eyes flickered and she straightened. "What phone call?"

"The one you made to your step-mother."

Rose stared at him, and her chin lifted fractionally. "But I told you, Chief Inspector; I didn't make one."

"I'm aware of that, miss. But it's been confirmed that a call was placed from this number at nineteen forty-three—nearly quarter to eight—that evening. It shouldn't be too difficult to—"

She raised both hands to her mouth, fingers splayed across her cheeks. Above them, her huge eyes were stricken.

"Perhaps if I ask your father or—"

"No!" Without warning she crumpled to the floor, hugging herself tightly and rocking backwards and forwards in an agony of despair. The policemen exchanged a startled glance. Then Webb motioned Jackson to the table and, bending down, lifted Rose to her feet. She collapsed against him, holding on to his lapels for support.

"Oh God, God, God!" she said rapidly.

"Now, now, miss. Suppose you calm down and tell me what it's all about."

"I killed her!" she said into his overcoat.

"I think you'd better start at the beginning."

"I didn't mean to! I never thought he'd hurt her. It didn't enter my head—"

"Who are you talking about, Miss Pendrick?"

She raised her ravaged face. "Danny. Danny Dean."

"Let's sit down, then, and you can tell me about it." He prised her fingers off his coat and led her to the sofa, manoeuvring her so that she was half-turned to face him, her back to Jackson. The Sergeant had taken out his pocket book. Rose seized Webb's hand and held on to it tightly.

"It was all so silly," she began, talking quickly in a low voice. "It started with Julian. Julian Bayliss. He was a boy I went round with for a while. Then he—he got a thing about Nancy. It was disgusting— she was old enough to be his mother. And she encouraged him." She broke off, then added honestly, "Well, I thought she did. It came to a head when I found them in here, kissing."

"Mrs. Pendrick and the boy?" Webb's surprise sounded in his voice.

"He probably took her by surprise. She looked rather startled. But you can imagine how I felt."

"You were fond of him?"

"Lord, no, but that's not the point. He was supposed to be in love with *me*. Nancy and I had a flaming row later. She said she *hadn't* encouraged him, but if anything that made it worse. So I accused her of cheating on my father, as well as spoiling my love-life."

"And what happened?" Webb prompted, as she came to a halt.

"A few days later, I overheard her

talking to Father. Her ex-husband had showed up at the hotel—as a barman, if you please! My hoity-toity stepmother and a barman! I'd been wondering how to get back at her, and it seemed too good to be true. So I went to have a look at him."

Her fingers tightened on his hand. "I told him who I was, and he thought it as funny as I did. 'Nance's stepdaughter!' he said. 'How do you like that?' And he asked me out for a drink."

Jackson rustled a paper, and Webb sent him a quick frown. But Rose was too absorbed with her story to notice. "We started going out. I liked him—he was amusing and quite attractive, really. It got more serious than I'd intended, but I thought I could finish it when I wanted to. We used to go to his room when he was off duty. He had one of the cottages in the grounds, so it was quite safe."

Webb waited patiently, his eyes on her lovely, downcast face. "Then something went wrong and he got the sack. I think he pinched some money, but I didn't hear the details. Actually, I was quite relieved. I'd been wondering how to end it, and it seemed the perfect solution. But he said he was looking for a job and digs in Shillingham, to be near me. It was a shock, I can tell you. I tried to talk him out of it, but he wouldn't listen. He was getting more intense all the time and I began to feel frightened. Then it was Christmas, and he sent me a gorgeous cashmere sweater. It must have cost a bomb—unless he pinched it. Anyway, I couldn't let it go on any longer. So I sent it back with quite a nice little note saying—well, you know —it had been fun while it lasted, but it was time he moved on. But he started ringing here, which he'd never done before. He didn't leave his name, but every time I came in, there were messages that someone had phoned. And when he couldn't get hold of me, he sent a letter, saying he'd never let me go."

"What did you do?"

"I threw it away. I thought he'd get the message and give up. But on the Tuesday after New Year, he was waiting for me at the gate. He was all wild-eyed and pale, and he grabbed hold of me and asked me to marry him. I was completely shattered. I tried to shake him off, but he wouldn't let go. Then he started slobbering over me. It was horrible, revolting. I was terrified someone would see us, but Danny said he'd go and tell Father we were engaged. I—well, I lost my head—screamed at him that he was an old man, and I wasn't going to marry my step-mother's cast-off. Honestly, I thought he was going to kill me."

She broke off with a shiver, realizing what she'd said. "He grabbed my arm and held it so tightly it hurt. He said he'd give me till the next evening, but if I didn't come to my senses by then, he'd come and get me. He said he knew I loved him, and was just playing hard to get."

She was silent for long seconds, staring at her fingers gripping Webb's hand. When she started again, her voice was shaking. "I was frantic—I didn't see how I could get through to him, and I knew he meant what he said. I daren't go to Father —he'd have gone mad if he knew what we'd been up to. Then it suddenly came to me. The one person Danny might listen to was Nancy. She was my last hope.

"I waited till she was home from work, then I phoned and told her the whole story. She was super—" Her voice broke.

"The nicest she's ever been to me. Not a word about what I'd done, or that it served me right, or anything. She said not to worry, she'd speak to Danny at the weekend. But I told her the weekend wouldn't do—he'd only given me till the next evening. So at last, to calm me down, she said, all right, she'd come back the next day and see him."

A tear plopped on his hand before he realized she was crying. "So I waited, all tensed up, for her to phone and tell me what had happened. She wasn't coming here, because we didn't want anyone to know about it. But when the phone went, it—it wasn't Nancy, it was Danny. Oh God!" she ended, on a little gasp.

Webb said steadily, "What time did he ring?"

She brushed her eyes with her hand. "About six, I suppose. Before dinner, anyway. His voice was all funny—I could hardly make out what he said. And when I did, I wished I hadn't. He said he'd been wrong about me, that I was a spiteful little whore, and if he ever caught up with me, he'd give me a dose of what he'd given Nancy." She was crying openly now, like a child, her face piteously crumpled. "I waited and waited for her to phone, and I tried to ring her several times. I couldn't think what had happened. Then when you came with Father to say she was dead— well, you can guess how I felt. And I didn't dare say anything, in case he killed me, too."

She collapsed against Webb, sobbing hysterically, her silky hair tickling his chin. The sex-kitten image had disintegrated and she was just a badly frightened young girl. He'd no reservations about putting his arm round her and patting her shoulder.

"All right, Rose, all right," he said at last, and none of them noticed he had used her first name. "You're a silly girl not to have trusted us, but we'll find him and nothing is going to happen to you. You've no idea where he's gone?"

She sniffed, shaking her head. Webb felt for a clean handkerchief and handed it to her. She blew her nose and sat up, pushing her hair back. Even in the aftermath of tears, she still looked lovely. Webb guessed not many women were so fortunate.

"London, I should think."

"You know what part?"

"He told me he came from Clapham."

"Right. We'll get on to the local Force." He didn't mention Crombie's theory; he was sure himself that Dean was alive, specially after that phone call. "Are you all right now?"

Rose nodded. Then she reached for his hand and held it against her cheek. "Thank you for being so nice."

Carefully he freed himself. "That's all right, miss. Now go and wash your face and try not to worry."

Jackson pushed back his chair and she turned sharply. As Webb had intended, she'd forgotten about the Sergeant, speaking freely on a one-to-one basis. But it was all safely down in Jackson's note-book, and after only a second's hesitation she obediently left the room.

13

THAT Jackson too had been struck by the girl's youth was reflected in his comment as they drove away. "Poor kid, her family doesn't seem to take much interest in her. No wonder she went off the rails." He paused. "Seems to put the lid on Dean's coffin, doesn't it? And you were right about Nancy's character doing for her. She must have gone at him hammer and tongs—well, we know that, from Mrs. Tallow—and he just snapped. Not wanting to foul his own nest, he followed her when she left, saw her turn down the alley, and—bingo!"

"And how did he get her to Chedbury without a car?"

Jackson grinned. "Come on now, Guv, I've solved most of it for you. Surely you can work that out!"

Webb grunted, then said suddenly, "Pull in here, Ken, will you." They were approaching the village centre. On their right, beyond the green, the little church sat atop its mound, its dark stone contrasting with the snow still lying in its shadow. On the left was the cobbled square with its specialist shops of which Webb disapproved.

"What is it, Guv? Fancy a bit of caviar?"

Webb sent him a withering look. "What was the name of the lad that fancied Nancy? Sounded like Bailey, but more highfalutin."

Jackson felt for his notebook and leafed through it. "Here we are. *Bayliss*. Julian Bayliss."

"Lord love us! Well, there's a phonebox over there, and by the look of it it's intact. Even has directories on the shelf. Nip in and look up his address, will you? Might as well see if he's home while we're in the area."

Minutes later, Jackson scrambled back into the car. "Only one lot locally, James R. Bayliss, The Fairway, Beckett's Lane. Must be further along from the Fraynes."

They drove slowly over the bridge, where an old lady was throwing bread to the ducks, passed the surgery with its two brass plates, and turned into Beckett's

Lane. The Fairway was the last house on the right, backing on the golf course. A young man was in the driveway, washing a car. He straightened as they drew up and came slowly down the path to meet them.

Webb got out of the car. The wind, skimming across the fields, stung his face. "Mr. Julian Bayliss?"

"Yes. You're the police, I suppose. I've been expecting you." He was stockily built, with neat reddish hair and hazel eyes reflecting the green of his sweater.

Webb looked past him at the house. "Is anyone at home?"

"My mother." The young man held his gaze.

"Would you prefer to talk out here?"

"Thanks. Yes, I would. Shall we walk down the road a bit?"

"Suits me."

Resignedly Jackson turned up his collar and fell in behind them as they walked in silence past the entrance to the golf club and along the cinder track into which Beckett's Lane had now degenerated. To their left a farm road, its deep ruts caked with ice, wound back in the direction of

246

the village, while ahead a five-barred gate set in a hedge effectively barred their way.

Webb rested his arms on it, eyes narrowed in the searing wind. "Right," he said, "this'll do." High overhead, a flock of rooks flew noisily towards some trees, and in the distance, borne towards them on the wind, came the whistle of a train. Jackson wondered fancifully if young Bayliss wished he were on it. The boy was staring out across the fields, but his shoulders were braced for the imminent questioning.

It began. "What do you do for a living, Mr. Bayliss?"

"I work for my father, sir. J. R. Bayliss and Son, Estate Agents. In Marlton."

"But not today?"

"I've been off this week, with flu, but I'll be back on Monday."

"You weren't ill on Wednesday the fourth?"

"No, sir." The boy shuddered, whether from cold or the significance of the date, Jackson couldn't be sure. "I was in the office all day. You can check," he added with a touch of defiance.

"We will, Mr. Bayliss, we will. Now,

what do you know about Mrs. Nancy Pendrick?"

"That she was the kindest, sweetest person I've ever met."

Here was a turn-up for the books. "Sweet" was a new adjective to be applied to Nancy.

"How well did you know her?"

"Not well enough. We'd very little time alone."

The implication that they'd both regretted this, Webb let pass for the moment. "You met through her step-daughter?"

"Yes. I was besotted with Rose. You'll have met her, so you'll understand. It was completely one-sided, of course, but it amused her to have me hanging around. 'My willing slave,' she called me. Well, Nancy—Mrs. Pendrick—saw what was happening. She was sorry for me, and went out of her way to be friendly. But then, to the surprise of all of us, I think, I—I fell in love with her. Everything I'd felt for Rose, and much, much more. Of *course* she was older in *years*, but her personality wasn't. She was bright and amusing and—and such good *fun*." He bit his lip.

Webb said woodenly, "Was your affection returned?"

"I honestly don't know. It might have been, in time. But Rose made an awful scene when she found us together. I think that's why Nancy withdrew. She didn't want anyone hurt—and there was also Mr. Pendrick to consider. I wrote her dozens of letters, but I tore them all up. It seemed so hopeless. *God*, how I wish I'd posted them—let her know I was serious about her. If we'd been together, none of this would have happened."

He really believed that, Jackson thought wonderingly. Poor, stupid little sod. Small wonder my Lady Rose had no time for him.

The boy said in a low voice, "You haven't found out yet, who—?"

"Not yet, I'm afraid."

"I wish to God they could still hang him!" He hit his forehead with his fist and held it there, eyes closed. When he opened them they were watering, but it could have been the wind.

Webb cleared his throat. "You've no

idea who might have a grudge against her, want her out of the way?"

"How could anyone? It must be a madman."

"You weren't at the Pendricks' on New Year's Eve, Mr. Bayliss. Were you invited?"

"No. I didn't expect to be."

"So when did you last see Mrs. Pendrick?"

"At one of the parties over Christmas—the Pipers'. But we didn't get a chance to talk."

Webb sighed. They hadn't got anywhere, but then he hadn't expected to. They'd check with his office as a matter of routine, then one more possibility could be scored through.

"Very well, Mr. Bayliss, that's all for the moment."

They turned and started to walk back to the house. Although snow lingered in the crevices, there was a steady dripping from the hedgerows as the sun grew stronger. Out on the golf course a group moved in slow motion, actors in a time-honoured ritual.

Jackson glanced surreptitiously at his

watch. Nearly midday. A bite of lunch would warm him nicely, he thought, brightening. At the gate of The Fairway they came to a halt.

"Thank you for your help, Mr. Bayliss," Webb said formally. "We'll be in touch if we need you again."

"Yes. Right." The boy hesitated, then thrust out his hand, which Webb solemnly shook. He turned to Jackson, who did the same. The two men got into the car, Jackson reversed in the driveway, and they drove back down the road. He could see the boy in the rearview mirror, standing looking after them.

"Reckon he really had flu, Guv?"

"Or something like it. Delayed shock. Often happens, that, after a death. Known medical fact."

"You mean he really was serious about her? At his age?"

"Come on, Ken. You're never more serious in your life than you are at twenty."

They had reached the main road and turned up the hill. "What now, then? Lunch?"

Webb smiled. "Yes, but not The Dog

and Gun. Let's find somewhere more in keeping with our pockets."

As they crested the hill and began to drop down the other side, leaving Frecklemarsh behind them, both men relaxed.

"Any plans for the rest of the day?" Jackson inquired.

"We must get on to Clapham about Dean, then there's a pile of paperwork needing my attention. Why?"

"Just that it's my lad's birthday. I'd like to get home early, if there's no panic on."

"Sure, why not?"

"Why don't you drop in yourself? Young Paul's a great fan of yours. It'd make his day, and Millie'd be pleased to see you."

"OK, Ken, thanks. I'll do that. And this looks a likely place for lunch."

Webb was an hour behind Jackson leaving Carrington Street, having stayed to read the reports. Not that there was much in them. They were in the doldrum stage which bedevilled most investigations, when nothing seemed to be happening. He

252

wanted Dean and he wanted Sharon, and so far both had eluded him.

Still, it was Friday evening and he'd earned a breather. He drew up outside the neat semi-detached on the Broadminster Road, smiling as he saw the balloons tied to the gate. How old would the kid be now? Six, seven? He was no good at judging children's ages—no experience.

The pavements glittered with frost and a new moon swung in the sky. The sound of children's voices floated down the path, and Mrs. Jackson opened the door, face flushed and hair dishevelled.

"Hello, Mr. Webb. It's good of you to come."

As he stepped inside, the door on the left burst open, enveloping them in noise, and Jackson stood there, holding a cake with smoking candles.

"Ah, there you are, Guv. Come on in. The cake's ready for cutting, love." He handed the plate to his wife and led Webb into the dining-room. The table down the centre was crowded with small boys, the sole exception being the host's five-year-old sister at one end. Distributed along it was a medley of cracker debris, abandoned sandwiches, plates of sausages on sticks.

"Dig in!" Jackson instructed. "Paul, here's Mr. Webb to say Happy Birthday."

"Happy Birthday, Paul," Webb repeated dutifully, and slipped a pound into the boy's pocket.

"Now look, Guv, that wasn't the idea at all. I didn't—"

"Rubbish. Can't come to a birthday party without a present, can I, Paul?"

The child said shyly, "Thank you, Mr. Webb." Unprompted, at that. Webb was quite impressed. He stood eating a sausage, watching the rosy, excited faces and feeling a rare touch of envy. This was a gap in his life he seldom thought about, but it would grow more noticeable as the years passed.

His brooding was interrupted by a fracas as fisticuffs broke out between the guests. Jackson separated them and grinned ruefully at Webb.

"Aren't you glad you haven't got kids?"

He'd been thinking the opposite, but he smiled and nodded. Even if he had, they'd live with Susan—that was the way things went. And kids were no insurance against old age. They might emigrate, then Ken'd be no better off than he was. Except that he'd have Millie, with her generous curves, her placid face and loving heart.

Catching his eye, she smiled at him, then clapped her hands.

"All right, boys. If you've had enough to eat, you can go and watch television."

There was a general stampede and the adults were left with the wreckage of the party. Millie laughed. "The blessings of the box! Until last year, we had to organize games for every minute they weren't eating."

There was a wail in the hall and young Vicky reappeared in the doorway. "Paul won't let me in!"

Jackson scooped her up in his arms. "You don't want to be with a lot of boys, do you? We're going to have a cup of tea, and if you're a good girl you can join us."

They sat at one end of the table, Vicky, thumb in mouth, on her father's knee, and Webb ate the statutory piece of cake.

Millie said quietly, "You're looking tired. It must be frustrating, when you can't get hold of people."

"Something'll break soon," he said,

with more confidence than he felt. "We've plenty of feelers out."

The telephone shrilled in the hall. She excused herself, reappearing a minute later. "It's for you, Mr. Webb."

He went quickly from the room. "Webb here," he said into the phone.

"Glad to have caught you, Guv." It was Fenton, the Desk Sergeant. "We've had Clapham on the line—they've traced the bloke you're looking for. Signed on today for unemployment benefit."

Webb stood quite still. "That's great, Andy. Thanks. Hang on while I find a pencil." Tucking the phone under his chin, he balanced his notebook on his knee and took down the address.

When he'd rung off, he paused for a moment, drawing a deep breath. Behind the living-room door a rattle of gunfire broke the enthralled silence. Out on the main road, a bus lumbered past. He slipped his notebook into his pocket and opened the dining-room door. Jackson looked up expectantly.

"Clapham," Webb said briefly. "The lull's over. Things are moving at last."

"And what did you do with yourself today?" Peter inquired, lavishly grinding pepper over his dinner.

Heather looked up, startled. "Nothing much. Why? You don't usually ask."

"Well, it's Friday the thirteenth, you know. I just wanted to check nothing untoward had happened."

She stared at him, hysterical laughter in her throat. "Everything's fine," she said.

"So it would appear. There's a positive aura of wellbeing about you this evening."

Beneath the table, her hands locked together. It seemed he noticed more than she'd thought. "Am I usually so glum, then?"

"Well, you have been edgy lately, haven't you? Ever since we came here, in fact. But I always said that, given time, you'd settle down and be happy. And I was right, wasn't I?"

"Yes, Peter, you were right."

Her mind slid to that afternoon, and her panic outside the café when, from being so desirable, her proposal seemed suddenly tawdry and cheap. All the concepts of honesty and fidelity by which she'd lived so far and to which, in her heart, she still conformed, rose about her like a swarm of wasps, enraged at their overthrowing.

She'd been on the point of turning away when the door was pushed open by an elderly gentleman, who stood aside for her to enter. And thank God she had. Thank God Oliver had understood. Thank God, thank God.

A vacant chalet in the hotel grounds, he'd said, approachable from the back road that ran from Beckett's Lane. No need even to go through the village. Monday afternoon.

"It makes it much easier for me," Peter was continuing, "knowing you're not fretting at home. You're even quite philosophical about Joey's going."

"I'm afraid I have been making heavy weather of it. I'll miss her, of course, but we can go down to see her, can't we?"

"Sure, and she'll be having long vacations for the next few years at least."

Heather's spirits soared irrepressibly. There was nothing she couldn't face, now that she had Oliver. And already Peter was appreciating the change in her. It was more than she deserved, but far from suffering from her love-affair, it would be to her husband's advantage.

"And you really are glad, after all, that we came to Frecklemarsh?" he persisted, stressing the wisdom of his decision.

"Of course I am," she answered dutifully, and smiled at him. "Very glad indeed."

14

THE more Webb saw of London, the more thankful he was to live in Broadshire. True, Shillingham had its dreary areas, notably around the station, but they were limited to a square mile or so, with the country only minutes away. Here, they seemed to have been driving for ever down dingy streets, past boarded-up shops, deserted factories and crumbling, decayed buildings. Yet it was here, even after a couple of months in Broadshire, that Dean had returned, felt most at home. No accounting for tastes.

A row of black plastic bags, put out for collection, had split to reveal the detritus of modern living. Tins, bottles and tea-leaves spewed over the pavement and were bowled along the gutters in the high wind. Down a side street, a market added to the dross its torn cabbage leaves and squashed tomatoes.

Jackson glanced at his chief's face.

"Come on, Guv, it's not that bad. 'All human life is here!'"

"And half of it under our wheels." Crowds were pouring across the street regardless of the slow-moving traffic, laughing, jostling, calling out to neighbours. A helmeted policeman stood benignly on the pavement, exchanging comments with the passers-by.

"How much further?" Webb asked, looking at his watch. This Saturday journey had already taken longer than their last, Sunday visit.

"Not far in miles, but at this rate the best part of half an hour. I don't know about you, but I'm hungry."

"When are you not, lad, but it's barely midday. We'll report to the local nick first; they're keeping tabs on Dean. No doubt they'll advise us on the availability of lunch."

Detective-Inspector Boon greeted them affably. "Hasn't shown his face yet and his curtains are still drawn. I'm not surprised, considering the time he hit the sack. Kept young Wilkins up till o-two hundred."

"How far away are his digs?"

"Just round the corner. Very handy."

"Then we'll avail ourselves of your interview room, given the chance."

"You want him for that body in the woods case?"

"We reckon he knows something, yes."

Jackson coughed discreetly, and Webb continued, "My sergeant here is dying of starvation. If the bird hasn't broken cover, we'll eat before tackling him. Where would you suggest?"

"The Pig and Whistle's quite reasonable. It's on the corner between here and Dean's place—halfway house, you might say."

"Will you join us?"

"Thanks, but no. I'm waiting for a phone call. If he makes a move, I'll send Sergeant Purvey after you."

The Pig and Whistle was four minutes' brisk walk from the station, and packed to the walls with lunch-time drinkers. Jackson's eagle eye spotted a couple vacating a table at the far end, and he managed to claim it while Webb placed their orders.

He was aware of excitement. Dean, their quarry almost since the beginning, was within a few hundred yards. Would his statement close the case? Stubbornly, Jackson was convinced it would. He'd discussed it with Millie the night before when, having cleared up after the party, they were sitting by the fire.

Millie had listened carefully, her knitting needles clicking a soothing accompaniment. "All the same," she said, when he came to an end, "he must know he's a suspect, being the last to see her. Why go back to his home ground without even changing his name?"

"A hunted animal returns to its lair," Jackson told her grandiosely. "Changing names takes time and money and Dean has neither. He needs unemployment pay, and that's what netted him." He was slightly aggrieved that she hadn't endorsed his reasoning. Millie had a sound head on her shoulders, and he valued her judgement almost as much as the Governor's.

He looked up to see Webb, head and shoulders above the crowd, weaving his way towards him. With the ease born of long practice, the Chief Inspector set down two brimming tankards without a drop being spilt.

"You need a survival course to face this

lot!" he commented. "Your turn, when the grub's ready."

Jackson had just laid down his fork with a sigh of satisfaction when Sergeant Purvey slid on to the bench next to him.

"You have company, gentlemen," he said in a low voice. "Dean's at the far end of the bar. Just closed his fist round a pint. Can't see him from here," he added, as Webb automatically turned. "He's wearing a blue anorak and red sweater. Want any assistance, sir?"

"He'd be hard pressed to make a dash for it," Webb commented. "However, if you'd stand by the door, Sergeant, you could escort us back with him."

The three men rose together, Purvey turning towards the door, Webb and Jackson walking down the length of the bar. Their first sight of Dean was two-sided, his back to them on the bar stool, bald patch inexpertly disguised; and opposite, in the mirror, the still-handsome face with high cheekbones and bright eyes. Some sixth sense alerted him, for he paused, glass half raised, and in the mirror his eyes met Webb's. He stiffened, then

264

sat unmoving as the Chief Inspector went forward.

"Mr. Dean?"

There was no answer and Webb continued, "Shillingham CID, sir. Chief Inspector Webb and Sergeant Jackson. We've a few questions to ask you."

Dean's colour faded patchily, white areas surrounding mouth and eyes. He looked quickly from side to side, assessing and rejecting any chance of escape. Then he said with forced jauntiness, "A fair cop, as you might say."

"If you'll accompany us back to the station, sir—"

"Shillingham?" He sounded startled.

"Not in the first instance. Farraby Road."

With a sigh, Dean relinquished his glass and slipped off the stool. Webb and Jackson closed in on either side and they made their way to the door. The incident had attracted no attention. All around them, shoulders were being slapped and stories exchanged; no one knew or cared that a man in their midst might be charged with murder.

As they stepped outside the wind

buffeted their faces, catching their breath and tossing it away, so that they gasped for air. Sergeant Purvey looked Dean up and down without speaking. Then, at a signal from Webb, he led the way to the Station.

Seated opposite Dean in the interview room, Webb guessed that last night's binge had been the rule rather than the exception. There were pouches under his eyes and his skin was loose and waxy.

"I'm cautioning you, Mr. Dean. You understand what that means?"

Dean nodded sullenly. "Any chance of a fag?"

"I don't smoke, but you're welcome to your own."

"Cheers." He fumbled for a battered packet and a box of matches. His fingers were grubby-nailed and brown with nicotine. Webb guessed they'd deteriorated since he worked at The Gables: possibly since he'd killed Nancy Pendrick.

"You know why we're here?"

The man drew on his cigarette. His previous experience with the law had taught him to volunteer nothing. "No."

"It concerns your ex-wife, Mrs. Nancy Pendrick."

Dean closed his eyes briefly. "I was sorry to hear about Nance."

"We have statements which suggest you were with her on the afternoon of her death. Is there anything you'd like to say?"

"As God's my witness, I didn't kill her." His voice was hoarse, and though any murderer would have said the same, Jackson thought: Hell's teeth, he's innocent. It was a gut feeling, impossible to justify, but his spirits, which had buoyed him up since yesterday's phone call, plummeted to rock bottom.

"Will you tell us, please, what happened that afternoon?"

Silence. Then Dean jabbed his cigarette in the ashtray and lit another. "It was that bloody girl's fault."

"Girl, sir?" Webb queried blandly, and saw tears well in the man's eyes. Dean slammed his hand on the desk.

"Godstrewth, a bloke my age! It's bloody pathetic, but I was so *sure*—well, it doesn't matter now. I was played for a sucker and that's all there is to it. An old man, she called me. Nancy's cast-off. How do you like that?" He brushed a hand fiercely across his eyes. "You married, Chief Inspector?"

"Not any longer."

"Wise man. 'The older they are, the harder they fall.' Isn't that what they say? I put the wind up her, though—I suppose that's something. She went bleating to Nance, who came charging back to sort me out." He gave a strangled laugh. "Typical, that is. Always thought she could tackle anyone. She learned different, though, didn't she?" He shielded his face with one hand.

Webb said quietly, "Mrs. Pendrick phoned you from London?"

"That's right. Said she wanted to see me."

"Did she say what about?"

"No, she sure as hell didn't. Thought it was for the sake of my blue eyes. Well, she'd got me off the hook at the hotel, hadn't she?" He wasn't bothering to be cautious now. "I wasn't expecting her to lam into me like that, and I lost my temper, too. Quite like old times, the pair of us bawling at each other. Old frozen-face must have got an earful."

"And what did she say?"

"Keep your dirty hands off Rose. Charming, when it was the little tart that made the running." His voice cracked and, knowing Rose, Webb could sympathize.

"I was crazy about her," Dean continued. He was beginning to enjoy himself, using his audience to talk away his heartache. "Even asked her to marry me, Gawd help me. But Nance wouldn't listen. Called me all sorts, and in the end I lashed out and caught her across the face. It was an accident—I hadn't meant to hit her—but she stormed off, threatening blood and thunder if I didn't stay away from Rose."

He stared down at the table, absently tracing its cracks with his nail.

"And then what happened?"

"I left, didn't I? Packed my bags and got out. I'd only stayed in the sticks because of Rose, and I wouldn't be seeing *her* again. So I caught the first train and came here. Mrs. Reith knows me from the old days, and doesn't ask questions."

"Did you make a phone call to Miss Pendrick?"

Dean looked sheepish. "I did, yes."

"Saying if you ever caught up with her, she'd get what you'd given Nancy?"

"Yes, well, I was still hopping mad. Not only that, I was *hurt*, dammit, to think she could—" He broke off, horror dawning in his eyes. "My God, she didn't think I meant—?"

"She did indeed."

"Rose thought *I'd* killed Nancy?"

"And that, given the chance, you'd do the same to her."

"Jesus!" he whispered, and it was more supplication than oath.

"What *were* you referring to, Mr. Dean?"

"The slap, of course. It was her that deserved it, not poor Nance, who'd only been doing her protective stepmother bit. When I—when I heard what happened, I'd have given anything to take it back."

Oliver Pendrick had said much the same.

"Where did you make the call from? Remember, we can check." But not easily, Webb thought wryly.

"Paddington. I'd been hashing over it all the way in, and I was pretty churned up. I reckoned it'd help if I told her what I thought of her."

Webb looked at him reflectively. He'd never been convinced Dean was their man; now he knew he was not.

"You read of her murder; why didn't you come forward?"

"Do me a favour! When I'd been heard yelling at her minutes before? When I'd got form, and just wriggled off the hook at the hotel? I was giving your lot a wide berth, I can tell you."

"You knew we'd be looking for you."

"Granted, but there was nothing I could say that would help Nance. Or you, for that matter, 'cos honest to God I don't know a thing."

There was silence, measured by the rhythmic ticking of the clock on the wall. When he could take no more of it, Dean said urgently, "You do believe me?"

"Yes, Mr. Dean, I think so."

Webb watched as relief illumined his face. "Straight up? Well, thank God for that! Can I go, then?"

"When you've signed your statement.

We'll get it typed now. And don't change your address without telling us, till the case is closed."

Dean sighed and leant back in his chair. "Well, that's a load off my mind, I must say." All at once, he looked years younger. He must have spent the last ten days looking over his shoulder, Jackson thought with grudging pity. But what a lot of time and trouble he'd have saved if he'd come forward in the first place.

"One thing more," Webb said smoothly. "Don't you owe Mrs. Tallow some rent?"

Dean flushed. "Well, she wasn't there, was she, and like I said I wasn't hanging about."

"That was ten days ago; you've had time to forward it, and I'm sure you'd like to start with a clean slate."

"Suppose so," Dean muttered.

Webb nodded, confident he would comply. "Sergeant, would you ask someone to type Mr. Dean's statement? Then I don't think we need detain him. Or ourselves, for that matter." He smiled. "Believe it or not, we're anxious to get back to the sticks."

Dean grinned, his cockiness already

restored. "Takes all sorts!" he commented.

"So there we are," Jackson said, breaking a long silence as they reached the motorway. "Back to square one."

"Not quite, but we'll have to do some rethinking. All along, we assumed that whatever brought Nancy to Broadshire had a direct bearing on her death. It looks as if we were wrong."

"Not necessarily, Guv. I mean, OK, so she came of her own accord, but someone must have known she was coming, and made use of it."

"But suppose we're barking up the wrong tree? What if her murder was more or less an accident, that she was just in the wrong place at the wrong time?"

Jackson said unbelievingly, "And the wrong time and place was four-thirty in Station Road?"

"Or the alley leading off it. And she saw something she shouldn't have done."

"Such as what?" Jackson's voice was flat, but his eyes glinted as they did when his interest was roused.

"God knows. There was no report of a

robbery or break-in. What could she have seen in those few minutes which was important enough to die for?"

"You're saying if she'd been five minutes earlier or later leaving Dean's place, she might still be alive?"

"I'm saying it's possible. We can forget Dean. He was the obvious choice, the ex-husband she'd just rowed with. It was too pat—I always thought that."

"There's still Pendrick. He wouldn't tell us where he was."

"If he'd been guilty, he'd have invented something. Oh, he'd the opportunity, but I don't go along with the motive—not if you're thinking of Mrs. Frayne. Mind you, he could have had an entirely different reason for killing her. We'll have to dig some more. Then there are the two who admit to being in Shillingham, Henry and Mr. Beresford. They accounted for their movements, but they could be lying. You know, Ken, I'm beginning to think the answer lies with that kid. Suppose what she said to Nancy led directly to her death?"

"If you're right, and the killer twigs it, she's in danger."

"Just what I was thinking. We'll arrange protection the minute she gets home."

It was six o'clock when they reached Carrington Street. "It's been a long day, Ken. You can knock off now."

"What about you, Guv?"

"I'm going to put a watch on the Robinsons' house. I want Sharon brought in the minute she gets back."

"You'll have a job shaking off the mother!"

"She can come if she wants—as far as the interview room. Not inside, though, and I shan't be, either. I'm counting on her talking more freely if there's only women present. Sally'll sort it out, with luck."

In his office, Webb put his plan into operation. "It may not even be tonight, Andy," he finished, "but whenever it is, I want to know the minute they get here with the girl. I'll hang on at The Brown Bear till closing time—you can bleep me there. After that, my home number."

At lunch-time and after work, The Brown Bear was like a club to Webb, crowded with friends and colleagues.

Now, on Saturday evening, it had an alien persona which the familiar surroundings served to emphasize. The faces round the bar were unknown to him: young people on their first date, couples filling in time before the cinema. He felt a stranger, as out of place as if he'd strayed into a different time-band.

He sat morosely at a table, staring into his beer and hoping his decision to guard Sharon Robinson wasn't too late.

"All alone, Mr. Webb?"

He looked up at the barmaid, engaged in emptying the ashtrays.

"Afraid so, Mabel. Waiting for a case to break."

"The murder?" A keen crime-follower, Mabel took pride in her police clientèle.

"Could be. Time to join me for a drink?"

"Well, I shouldn't, but the rush is over for the moment. Ta."

He watched as she had a word with the barman and returned with her usual Bloody Mary.

"Bottoms up, Mr. Webb!"

He raised his glass to her and drank, watching her over the rim. A peroxide blonde in her fifties, she was lavishly made up and exuded a cloying scent of tea-rose. Her silky open-knit top was hard put to support her heavy breasts, and at the station they placed bets on the number of bangles she wore. But for all her blowsiness, her brown eyes were warm and concerned.

"Getting you down, is it, this murder?"

"All murders get me down, Mabel."

"Get away—you thrive on them! I watched the replay on telly. Quite a thrill, seeing old Shillingham on the box. Did you get anything out of it?"

"That's what I hope to find out."

And right on cue, the bleeper sounded in his pocket. The barmaid's eyes widened in excitement. "What's that, then?"

"The information I've been waiting for." He finished his drink, wiping the back of his hand across his mouth. "Sorry, Mabel, I must go. See you Monday, all being well."

He stood up, his tiredness dropping away, and leaving her staring after him, made his way out of the pub.

15

"THIS really is the limit!" Mrs. Robinson said indignantly. "We've had a long journey, and the last thing we want is to be dragged out at this time of night. If this is what I get for doing my duty and bringing Sharon to see you, I'll know better next time."

"I'm sorry, Mrs. Robinson, we'll be as quick as we can. And I did say there was no need for you—"

"Let her go by herself? The very idea! A disgrace, I call it. I've a good mind to write to my MP."

"That's your privilege," Sally said quietly. She hoped the Governor knew what he was doing. The kid seemed terrified; just as well Liz was with her in the back—she looked as if she could pass out. Then the cat *would* be among the pigeons.

With relief, she saw they were turning into Carrington Street. Now she'd only to extract Sharon from her mother's clutches, and leave the latter to Andy.

It was easier than she'd expected. In the formal atmosphere of the foyer, Mrs. Robinson's defiance wilted. She heard Andy say bracingly, "Now, ma'am, I'm sure we could rustle up a cup of tea."

Sharon hadn't uttered a word in their presence. Somehow, that silence would have to be broken.

"Perhaps you'd like some tea, too?" she began.

The girl shook her head, and after a moment said, "No, thanks."

"Sharon, I'm sorry to bring you here. I know you're tired, but it's very important. I want you to tell us again what happened on the fourth of January."

"Mum had run out of flour. She sent me to fetch some."

"And?"

The girl licked her lips. "On the way back I fell and hurt myself. The lady helped me up, and then I went home."

"That's not quite all, is it?"

"I told them what she said. It was nothing important."

"How about what you said to her?"

It was impossible for the child's face to become paler, but her eyes were hunted. "I don't remember."

A direct approach seemed indicated. "Why were you in the alley?"

Sharon gasped. For a moment she stared at the policewoman. Then, bursting into tears, she covered her face with her hands. Sally moved round the desk and put an arm round her. "There's nothing to be afraid of. No one's going to hurt you, but you must tell us *everything*."

Sharon said from behind her hands, "Will you tell Mum?"

"Only if it's necessary."

"I didn't mean to do anything wrong."

Sally sat down again. "Suppose you start at the beginning."

The girl felt for a handkerchief and blew her nose. It seemed that, faced with the inevitable, the truth would after all be a relief. "I went to the Co-op and got the flour. When I came out, I saw two boys I know across the road." A tinge of colour seeped into her face. "They called me over, so I went."

"Go on."

Sharon bit her lip. "Do I have to tell you?"

"I think you should." Though God knows how this adolescent skirmishing concerned Nancy Pendrick.

"They were fooling around, pushing each other about. Steve said to Jonathan, 'You said you fancied her, now's your chance. I dare you to take her down the alley!' I tried to edge past, but Steve grabbed my arm. He said, 'You like Jonathan, don't you, Sharon? How about a nice cuddle?'"

Her face was bright red now, and she stared at her hands twisting the handkerchief. She added wistfully, "And I *do* like him, so I said all right. Mum'd *kill* me!"

Sally felt a stirring of pity, remembering the traumas of youth.

"It was dark down there," Sharon went on shakily. "There aren't many lamps. I let him kiss me and he—put a hand inside my jumper. Then all of a sudden he froze. I turned round, and I—I saw a man in one of the gateways, watching us. Jonathan said loudly, 'Dirty bastard! Can't you get your own kicks?' And he ran off, calling me to follow him. I started to, but my legs were all wobbly and I tripped." She looked up, meeting Sally's eye. "That bit was true, but it happened earlier. The man caught me and stopped me falling. I started to scream, but he said quickly, 'I'm sorry—I didn't mean to frighten you.' He talked posh, like they do on the news, so I thought it was all right."

The tears welled again and spilled down her cheeks. Sally waited while she mopped them with the crumpled handkerchief.

"But then he—he said he'd like to touch me, too, and if I let him, he'd give me five pounds."

Sally stared at her. Suddenly the story had taken a serious turn. Child molesting? Was that what Nancy had stumbled on?

"He took out the money and put it in my pocket. I knew I shouldn't, but he was so nice and polite. It didn't seem much for five pounds. But he—he didn't do it like Jonathan, and he started breathing all funny-like, and I got scared and ran away."

"And bumped into Mrs. Pendrick?"

"Yes. She asked what was wrong, and I told her. Then I ran home. I was afraid he'd come after me."

"He didn't force himself on you?"

"No. He just kept saying, 'Please—please—' in a kind of whimper." She shuddered. "It was horrid. I keep dreaming about it."

"Can you describe him, Sharon?"

"I didn't see his face, it was too dark. But he smelt piney." Some identity parade, with the witness sniffing all their after shaves.

Sharon said again, "You won't tell Mum, will you?"

Sally hesitated. "I'll have to check on that, but she wouldn't blame you. It's something that could happen to anyone."

"She'd ask why I was there in the first place."

"How old are you, Sharon?"

"Thirteen and a half."

"Which school do you go to?"

"Dick Lane Comprehensive."

"Were Jonathan and Steve there when you came out of the alley?"

"I didn't see them."

Bloody boys, leaving her alone like that!

A sudden thought struck Sharon, and she said in alarm, "You won't tell on them, will you, at school?"

"I shouldn't think so. But I hope you've learnt—" Sally broke off. Sharon patently *had* learned her lesson, and no amount of moralizing could stamp it any deeper. She said more gently, "Thank you for telling us. I know it wasn't easy, but it's helped a lot."

"Was it him that killed the lady?"

"I don't know."

She shuddered again. "He might have killed *me*!"

"Yes, he might. Never take such risks again."

She glanced at Liz with raised eyebrows, and was answered by a nod. "You'll have to sign your statement, Sharon—all the things you've told us—but we won't keep you now. Try to forget about it for the moment."

As the door opened Mrs. Robinson came to her feet, eyes raking her daughter's tear-stained face. Sally said quickly, "Thank you, Mrs. Robinson, Sharon's been very helpful. Constable Trent will drive you home."

And with a dismissive smile, she turned and ran up the stairs to Webb's office. He was waiting with the door open.

"Well?"

"You were right, sir, it could be important. She met a groper down there. I don't think it went any further. Sharon said he was a gentleman and she didn't realize what he wanted. He gave her five pounds."

"Ye gods! And she told Nancy?"

"Yes."

"Who, still steamed up about Rose and Dean, took on Sharon's cause too. Dean said she'd tackle anyone."

"And since he was keyed up and frustrated, he killed her?"

"It seems so, though sexual assault would have been more likely."

"Perhaps he only likes little girls."

"Perhaps. Anything else of interest?"

"Not really. She'd gone there with a boyfriend for a spot of petting, and the bloke was watching them. The boy ran off but Sharon stumbled and was left behind."

"And he abandoned her?"

"Charming, isn't it?"

"He needs whipping. She could have been murdered."

"Are you giving her protection?"

"I've arranged it, yes. If this *was* the

285

killer and he thinks she could recognize him, he might go after her. The murder could have pushed her from his mind till the recap on TV, and she's been away since it was shown. He might be hanging round waiting for his chance. Is the statement being typed?"

"Yes, sir, but I didn't make them wait. I wasn't sure what Mrs. Robinson would come out with, and the kid had had enough."

"Fair enough. OK, Sally, thanks. Enjoy what remains of the weekend."

For some moments after she'd gone, Webb stared broodingly down at his desk. Against its polished surface, mental images came and went, half-memories, crystallizing briefly and then fading. He needed to set it down in black and white, to compile a visual aid which might, as so often in the past, point him to the right conclusion. Tomorrow was Sunday; weather permitting, he'd set off with his easel and, by building up a detailed picture of what he knew, try to arrive at the answer they were all seeking—who killed Nancy Pendrick.

But the weather was against him. When he drew back his curtains the next morning, fog pressed against the pane. There was nothing for it but to work at home.

Up in his eyrie Webb cooked eggs and bacon, while in the street below cars crawled along blindly, tooting at every corner. Normally from here he'd a view of gardens falling away to the foot of the hill. Today, he couldn't see the garage in the drive beneath.

He turned the eggs, impatient to start work. There were enough facts to make an educated guess; proving it would be another matter.

Tipping the food on to a plate, he sat down at the table. Beside him, still unfolded, lay yesterday's local paper, and as he sipped his coffee he opened it to see Roger Beresford smiling up at him.

BROADSHIRE MAN HIGH COURT JUDGE ran the headlines. So he'd made it. Good for him. Lady Muck would be pleased. Pushing away the paper, Webb finished his breakfast.

Ten minutes later the easel was set up, the crayons to hand and he was ready to begin. He started by drawing the section of the town from which Nancy disappeared, marking in the relevant places. At the top right of the sheet was the station and in front of it the car park which Henry had used. Just below came Jubilee Road, Nancy's last port of call, and, a little further down, Wellington Street, home of the Robinsons. Then the Punjabi Gardens beside the alley, the bookmakers', and, on the corner of Gloucester Circus, the Odeon cinema.

Webb studied it for several minutes before filling in, on the left, the pawnshop and the Co-operative Stores. Radiating from the Circus like wheel spokes, he duly named Carlton Road, East Parade, Duke Street and the High Street. Each of them was mentioned in the statements, for into this small area had come that afternoon the actors in the drama: Nancy, Dean, Henry, Sharon, the Beresfords, Pussy Barlow. Perhaps, also, Oliver Pendrick? And what of Julian Bayliss? The story might not be as he told it and they still hadn't checked his alibi. Suppose he'd blurted out his love and Nancy'd laughed at him? Ridicule could be a powerful motive. So which of them had stood in the shadows watching the young lovers?

Dean could be eliminated. A check on timetables showed that to phone from Paddington at six, he must have caught the four-fifty. There was no way he could have packed his things, killed Nancy, dumped her body, and still made the train.

Moving on to the next name, Webb considered Henry. What had been his mood that day—worried about money, resentful of having to pawn his things? And it was Nancy's refusal of help that brought him to Shillingham. Suppose that, coming on the petting session, he'd over-reacted? The girl was closest to him in age; in the dark, not to mention the circum-stances, he could well have thought her older. And if Nancy of all people came storming round the corner—and recog-nized him—he might, in a panic, have killed her.

Or were they wrong to link the killer and Sharon's "gentleman"? They might be two separate people who had passed in the alley, little guessing they'd be merged into one in the mind of officialdom.

Webb tore off the sheet and it floated

to the floor as he started on the *dramatis personae*. Within minutes, he'd peopled the page with startling likenesses of the Pendricks and their friends: Oliver with his thick hair, the bump in his nose exaggerated as were all caricatures; Henry, thin and nervous; Beresford, whom, for his own amusement, Webb decked out in wig and gown; and Rose—beautiful, heartless Rose, who'd encouraged poor Dean in his daydreams and who, by bringing Nancy to Shillingham, had inadvertently caused her death.

Around him, Sunday life went on. The family at No. 5 returned from church; in No. 3, Hannah, unaware Webb was in the building, roasted her beef and ate alone. And still, isolated by the fog, wrapped in an eerie solitude, he worked on, while the muffled afternoon darkened to evening. It was there, he felt, if only he could spot it, the discrepancy which would shake the kaleidoscope of facts into a new pattern. Someone had lied. Who, and in what respect?

At five, in response to his growling stomach, he stopped for food. A gentleman, Sharon had said. Apart from

Dean, they all spoke well. Pity she'd been so vague on descriptions. They hadn't even tied down age, though to a child of thirteen that was at best relative.

He ate standing at the window, his reflected image staring back from the opaque darkness. At breakfast he'd been eager to start, confident of reaching the right conclusion. Now, more than eight hours later, he was tired and dispirited. But he might as well face it, no convenient tramp would materialize and confess. There, on this sheet of paper, he'd already drawn the murderer. He had only to take off his blinkers to see who it was. Personally, he felt he'd do better with a pin.

He rinsed his plate under the tap and left it on the draining-board. Perhaps the confines of the room constricted him. Perhaps he needed the openness of fields and sky for his mind to roam free. Excuses, excuses, he thought, sitting at the easel. For ten, fifteen minutes, he stared at his drawing, till its lines blurred and separated into black dots. He blinked, rubbed his eyes and picked up a crayon.

Start again, then. Go over it from the

beginning, and by heaven if there was anything there, he'd find it.

Henry first. Crayon in hand, Webb traced the boy's route from the station car park. He'd have crossed the road about—here—and gone into the pawnshop. Then, according to his statement, he'd walked round the corner into the High Street. He mentioned Boots, which was about here, and Payne's the shoe shop. That was quite a way along.

Webb stared frowningly at the cross marking the position of the shoe shop. Just beyond it was Dick Lane, which linked the High Street with Station Road and came out opposite the station. Surely, with his parking time running out, Henry'd have taken the short cut back instead of returning via the Circus?

Webb felt a sudden tingling on his scalp. *But Beresford had seen him!* Knocking over the stool in his haste, he reached for his pocket-book, flicking rapidly through its pages in search of the Pendricks' phone number. Seconds later Henry, sounding surprised, confirmed his assumption. He had not returned to the Circus, but cut through Dick Lane back to the car. The only time he'd have been visible from the cinema was when he left the pawnshop around four-fifteen.

Webb replaced the phone and stared down at it, his mind racing. God, no! he thought instinctively. Not *Beresford*! He went back to the easel, righting the stool as he unwillingly pursued the new train of thought. But there was no disputing that if, as he said, he'd seen Henry, Beresford must have come out of the cinema a good forty-five minutes earlier than he claimed. So why had he lied? Because his alibi depended on timing? Because it was he who had turned down the alley *en route* for the car park, stopped to watch Sharon and her boyfriend, and—?

If Nancy had stormed round the corner, coming face to face not with Henry but with *Roger*—what then? Webb stared at the bewigged cartoon, imagining his pleas. But an imminent judgeship wouldn't silence Nancy.

He thought back to the Chelsea interview. "I've seen the film three times—not much of an alibi." Could Beresford have been so honest if he'd needed that alibi?

Perhaps the ability to act, to disguise his

feelings, was inherent in his profession. Webb would only know for sure after seeing him.

He tidied his work away. For the first time he could remember, he regretted the conclusion it had led to. Dammit, he *liked* the man, respected him. Oddly, he found it easier to accept him as a murderer than as pervert. Still, thank God, it wasn't his place to judge him.

In the kitchen he picked up the paper again, staring down at the smiling face. Then, dropping it on the table, he turned away. Though tired of his own company, it was pointless to venture out in the foggy darkness. Still, if Hannah was home—

He phoned down, his spirits lifting as she answered. "Can you spare a few hours for a weary copper?"

"Of course. I was just thinking about you."

"Be with you in five minutes," he said happily, and hung up.

16

JACKSON stared at him in horror. "*A High Court Judge? In an identity parade?*"

"I'm afraid so, Ken. Let's see what aftershave His Lordship uses. But first we'll pop round to the school and see Sharon. There's her statement to be signed, and she might have remembered something."

Dick Lane Comprehensive was in the small road which had proved Beresford's undoing. There was ironic justice there. The school had started life as a Secondary Modern, expanding to embrace the buildings on either side when it aspired to Comprehension. The result, to Webb's eyes, was sprawling and makeshift.

As they drew up outside, he caught sight of WDC Day at a discreet distance. With luck, she'd soon be relieved from duty.

The Headmaster was a small, self-important man, whose timetable made no provision for police visits. He showed them to his study, and left them while he dispatched someone to find Sharon.

Jackson shifted his feet uncomfortably. The smell of chalk and ink and young bodies evoked in him a powerful sense of recall. How often had he stood in such a room, regretting skipped homework, owning up to broken windows, hoping to deflect a bad report—never, it seemed, for any pleasant purpose. No prizes or commendations had come his way, but he hadn't been seen by the police, either.

His reminiscence was broken by a tap on the door and Sharon came in. To Webb's relief, she seemed more composed than when he'd last seen her. Perhaps, having confessed her misdemeanours, she'd resolved to forget them.

"We've brought your statement along," he said pleasantly. "Will you read it through, please, and then sign it?"

They waited in silence while she went through the typed sheets, a frown of concentration between her eyes. There was a smudge of ink on her cheek and in her grey skirt and jumper she looked touch-ingly young. Webb's heart hardened against her molester.

She looked up. Reading the statement didn't seem to have distressed her. "Yes, that's right," she said.

"Then will you sign it, please?"

He handed her his pen and she leant on the desk to write, her single heavy plait swinging over her shoulder.

"Thank you." He took the papers from her and passed them to Jackson. "Now, Sharon, we're arranging an identity parade. You know what that is?"

She nodded. "I've seen them on telly."

"The men will repeat in turn the words that were said. You might recognize a voice. Have you remembered anything since you spoke to Miss Pierce?"

"I don't think so."

Webb thought of Roger Beresford. What was his most distinguishing feature? The lock of hair falling over his brow? He said on impulse, "I know it was dark, but concentrate for a moment. You must have noticed *something*, even if subconsciously. His hair, for instance. Was he bald?"

She stared at him, memory stirring at

the back of her eyes. "No. I remember now, it flopped over his face."

Webb drew a deep breath. It wasn't much, but it was something. "Anything else?"

"No, except that he talked nice."

"All right, Sharon, thank you. That's all. We'll be in touch when everything's arranged."

Jackson was glad to leave that study, with its registers and exercise books. Schooldays hadn't been the happiest of *his* life, that's for sure.

"Off to London, then?" he asked, as Webb fastened his seat-belt.

"Yep. The car should know its way by now. Still," he added grimly, "it'll be the last time, on this case at least."

"He might be in Surrey," Jackson suggested.

"Not mid-week. Anyway, the *News* said he's attending a function this evening. God, Ken, I'm not looking forward to this."

Roger said, "Hello, Charlotte. It's good of you to come."

"A pleasure—I can congratulate you in

person. Well done, Roger, it's splendid news and well-deserved."

"Let me take your coat."

She walked ahead of him to the drawing-room, stopping in surprise to find it empty. "Where's Faith?"

"Having her hair done, for tonight's dinner. There's coffee on the tray, if you'd like to pour."

Charlotte glanced at him curiously. There was an air of detachment about him that she couldn't quite gauge. Perhaps, she thought, amused, he was practising for his elevated position. Roger set great store by appearances.

She poured from the silver coffee-pot. The cups, she noted, were Crown Derby. "Well, what's all this about? Why the urgent request to see me?"

He didn't answer at once. He took the cup and saucer from her, absent-mindedly stirring though, as she knew, it was years since he'd taken sugar.

"I needed to talk, Charlotte, and apart from Avis you're the only one I've ever been able to talk to. You don't mind?"

"Of course not. What do you want to talk about?"

"Old times," he said, surprising her. "I was remembering, as we drove over at New Year, all those Christmases when we were young. They were good times, weren't they?"

"Very good, yes." Charlotte was puzzled. Had he brought her fifty miles to talk about the past?

"It did snow, didn't it, when we went carol-singing? They say we've had few white Christmases this century, but I don't believe it."

"I'm sure it snowed." Her eyes were on his face.

"And then, when we were older, all those parties and dances." He smiled reminiscently. "That's when I fell in love with you." He looked at her with the shy diffidence he'd never outgrown. "I really did love you, you know."

"And I you," she said gently. "Just not enough for marriage."

"Not enough," he echoed. "The story of my life. Only Avis loved me enough. God, how I miss her!"

Charlotte moved uneasily. He was in a strange mood and she doubted the reason he'd given for her summons. Nevertheless, something inside her was responding to his need and, uncertain why he needed comfort, she tried to offer it.

"Twins are special, of course, but you underestimate the rest of us. Your parents, for instance—"

"They started it. They were always hugging and kissing Avis, but if I climbed on someone's knee, I was put down and told to be 'a little man'. Odd, how that's stayed with me all these years."

"But it didn't mean anything," Charlotte protested, wondering why, after forty-odd years, she must now defend the Beresfords. "In those days, people thought little boys—"

"And I needed it far more than she did —to be held close and told I was loved. How else could I know? To me, touching's an essential part of loving." He sighed. "Not to everyone, though. Faith for one loathes me 'pawing' her, as she calls it."

Charlotte said gently, "Why are you telling me this?"

"Because I need someone to understand."

"Understand what?"

"Me," he answered simply. "Bear with

301

me, Charlotte, it's important. I'm just saying I've been held at arm's length all my life. Avis apart, the only spontaneous love I've had has been from children—particularly Rose."

He was silent, staring across the room into a past Charlotte couldn't after all share. Beneath her pity, unease was growing.

Roger smiled suddenly. "When she was little, I sometimes used to bath her. I still dream of that sturdy little body, and the way she'd fling her arms round my neck and hug me. She couldn't have known what it meant to me. Oh, it wasn't sexual—I hope I needn't add that—just sheer animal touching, an expression of belonging. Then, of course, she grew up and the contact was broken.

"Still—" he straightened his shoulders —"there have been compensations, my career for one. My career." He paused, then went on, "I was desperate to prove myself, and since people are impressed by success, I hoped that might do the trick. I thought it had worked when Faith married me, but I was wrong. Oh, she's *fond* of me. She enjoys having a rich and

302

successful husband, but she doesn't want me in her bed."

Charlotte said abruptly, "Do you mind if I smoke?" Her fingers shook as she extracted a cigar from her case. Ever the gentleman, Roger came over with a light. His hand, too, was shaking. God, she thought suddenly, what am I *doing* here?

He returned to his chair and, bending over its arm, retrieved a pocket recorder. Charlotte said sharply, "What's that for?"

"Ignore it, if you can. What I'm saying could be of interest to a psychologist."

"Roger, is there something seriously wrong?"

He laughed with genuine amusement. "You could say that."

"Then tell me, so I can help."

"That, Charlotte, is what I'm doing."

There was a febrile excitement about him which reminded her of his dead sister and stirred into life all the uncomfortable feelings she'd once had for him—tenderness, protectiveness, and a helpless, unwilling irritation. She glanced at her watch, wondering how soon Faith would be back.

"Oddly enough," he went on, "I was

thinking of Rose that afternoon in the cinema. A child there looked much as she had at seven or eight. And suddenly everything I've been talking about welled up inside me. I suppose, to be coldly factual, it was an orgy of self-pity. I did my best to fight it, listing all the successes I'd had, and so on; but I'd have traded the lot for one person who unreservedly loved me. The cinema was hot and I couldn't concentrate on the film—I knew it by heart, anyway. My stomach was churning and I had to get out.

"I stood on the steps for a while, drawing deep breaths of cold air. It was then I saw Henry." He smiled wryly. "I shouldn't have mentioned that. Never elaborate: how often have I drummed that into my clients? It'll strike them eventually that the timing doesn't fit. Perhaps it already has."

"Strike whom?" Charlotte asked out of a dry mouth. Was he mentally ill? Was that what he meant about a psychologist?

"The police."

"The—?" She leant forward urgently, incredible ideas colliding in her head. "Roger, what are we talking about?"

"The day Nancy died."

She stared at him whitely. "What has Nancy to do with this? Were you in love with her?"

"God, no. She's *nothing* to do with it— nothing. That's the tragedy."

"I don't want to hear any more." The reason for the recorder was suddenly, appallingly, evident and her fear for him exploded into anger. "You've no right to use me as Father Confessor."

"The right of friendship, Charlotte? Won't you accept that?"

She ground out her cigar. "Go on, if you must."

"Thank you. As I was saying, I saw Henry. He came out of a seedy-looking shop and walked round the corner into the High Street. The town clock was chiming the quarter past four. Faith wouldn't be finished at the hairdresser's for another hour."

He smiled suddenly. "Strange, isn't it? At the most crucial moments of my life, my wife is at the hairdresser's! There must be a moral somewhere. Anyway, I decided to go for a drive and sort myself out. But on the way to the car park, I came across

305

a young couple kissing. They were in that alleyway—you know the one?"

Charlotte nodded.

"I moved back against the wall and watched them for a while. The girl's head was back and the boy's hand inside her coat. Touching."

Charlotte sat unmoving.

"I must have been staring too hard. The boy raised his head and saw me. He shouted some filth—frightened, I suppose —and set off for the main road. The girl started after him, but she stumbled and would have fallen if I hadn't caught her. That was all I meant to do, but the warm, living feel of her, her breathing still quick from the boy's kisses—it ignited everything inside me. She seemed to turn into Rose, who in her innocence had let me touch her.

"I don't know what I said—it's a merciful blur. I gave her money—I remember that—and I started to caress her. At first she didn't object. Then, as I grew excited, she became frightened and ran away. I didn't hurt her, Charlotte, I swear it. Even if she'd stayed, I shouldn't have gone further. But she ran away."

He wiped a hand across his brow, pushing back the soft hair. "God knows, if I'd been in my right mind I'd have got the hell out myself, but I literally couldn't move. I just clung to the wall, unable to believe what had happened. And the next minute, Nancy came charging round the corner in search of me. Or rather, in search of the monster who'd molested the child."

"Oh God!" Charlotte breathed. "No!"

"You know, until I saw the recap on TV I hadn't realized how young the girl was. Not that I thought about it, I was past being rational. And you can imagine Nancy's attitude—self-righteous to the last." He paused. "God, that was apt, wasn't it? I tried to bluster, of course, but she could see the state I was in and she just let fly. I made no attempt to stop her—I agreed with everything she said. But she was still haranguing me when some people turned into the alley, and the last thing I wanted was an audience. So since she wouldn't stop ranting, I took her arm and led her to the car park.

"My car was at the far end, away from the others. By this time, I was trying to calm her down, but I was far from calm myself. I told her I'd been appointed a judge, but that didn't weigh with her. She replied—quite rightly—that I wasn't fit to judge anyone. I tried to explain, but she wouldn't listen. She raved on and on, accusing me of all kinds of perversion, and suddenly I'd had enough. Also, there were people at the far side of the car park, and her voice was rising."

Out in the square a car door slammed and someone laughed. Footsteps went lightly up the steps next door. Ordinary people, doing ordinary things on an ordinary Monday morning. With an effort, Charlotte unclenched her hands. There was no way of stopping him now. Just as, ten days ago, there'd been no way of stopping Nancy. Except one.

"I put my hands round her neck and shook her, just to make her stop. But almost immediately she went slack. I must have pressed on some vital point, I don't know. Perhaps she had brittle bones. She slumped to the ground and I thought she'd fainted. I even tried to revive her. It was several minutes before I realized she was dead." He paused, then added tonelessly,

"I'm not entirely sure that's true. I don't *think* I meant to kill her, but I had to keep her quiet. Not only then, in the car park, but later. Especially later. And when I realized that she *was* dead, my first feeling was relief."

Charlotte was incapable of breaking the silence. She stared at him till her eyes ached, this man she'd known forty years, as brother, lover, friend. A man whose need to be loved had finally led him to murder.

He moved at last. "I panicked, naturally. In half an hour I was due to pick up Faith. I bundled Nancy into the car and set off for the nearest open country. When I saw the Chedbury sign, I remembered the woods. I—left her there and drove rapidly back, parking in the same car park but not, I assure you, in the same part of it. And I met Faith and somehow, God knows how, pretended nothing had happened.

"I told myself it was an accident; I hadn't meant to kill her, so I shouldn't be punished for it. She might even have had a heart attack—she was worked up enough. I couldn't believe that the seconds

I'd held her neck were enough to kill her. She didn't even try to move my hands. And I bargained with myself that I'd be a better person from now on. I'd put myself out to help people—all the usual, puerile attempts to placate the avenging furies. But it didn't work. They were in my head, and they wouldn't go away. I've spent too long in the courts for that kind of self-deception."

Charlotte said without hope, "What will you do?"

"You know as well as I do. There must be the minimum publicity, for Faith's sake."

Seeing her stricken face, he added gently, "Don't look like that, Charlotte, it's only the *coup de grâce*. In all respects that matter, my life ended when I turned into the alley, as surely as Nancy's did. This is just a formality, 'a necessary end'."

"But there must be *something*—"

"No," he contradicted gently, "nothing. Forgive me for inflicting this on you, I needed the strength."

"But there are mitigating circumstances! A moment's madness, that's all it was— first the girl and then, by the sheerest bad luck, Nancy. What was she doing in Shillingham, anyway? She'd no right to be there!"

"Charlotte, love, don't."

"You know all the leading Counsel. Surely—"

"Death," he said simply, "will be much easier." He switched off the recorder and, coming towards her, drew her to her feet and into his arms. When had he last held her close? All those years ago, in Beckett's Lane, when she'd ended their relationship? She'd been as guilty as anyone of rejecting him. But love can't be made to order—one of the tragedies of human existence.

Now, in rebuttal of the thought, she was filled with a desolation that could surely be no deeper had she truly loved him. Kind, gentle, over-affectionate Roger, cast as murderer. There was after all no justice, despite his having spent his life administering it.

But it was her strength, not her sympathy, he asked of her, and she mustn't fail him now. Closing her mind to the bitterness and tears that would come later, she held him tightly, trying to transmit the courage he needed. Perhaps it came through, because after a few minutes he patted her arm and released her. His face was composed, the feverish excitement gone.

"Bless you, Charlotte," he said quietly. He picked up the recorder and put it into her hand. "Give that to the Chief Inspector. Faith won't be coming back here—I sent her a message—and you mustn't either, though the door won't be locked. Go down the steps and walk quickly away. Try not to think too harshly of me."

He brought her coat, helped her into it, showed her to the door. They might have been casual friends, meeting again in a couple of days. Charlotte turned to face him, owing him the courage he displayed himself.

"Goodbye, Roger. I'm proud to have known you." She reached up and kissed him. Then she went obediently down the steps. Behind her, she heard the door close.

The uncaring sunshine poured into the square. On one of the railings a fat little robin preened its feathers. She stood for a moment watching it, turning her head as a car drove swiftly round the corner. It contained the Chief Inspector and his sergeant.

Webb seemed concerned to see her and, barely waiting for the car to stop, got out and hurried towards her. Wordlessly, she held out the recorder, and as he took it, a muffled shot rang out, rattling the windows behind them.

The robin, startled, flew away.

THE END

૧૨૪
૧૫૧